The Healer

SEAGULL
BOOKS
•
CELEBRATING
40 YEARS

THE SLOVAK LIST

OTHER TITLES FROM THE SLOVAK LIST

Boat Number Five

MONIKA KOMPANÍKOVÁ

Translated by Janet Livingstone

The Thankless Foreigner

IRENA BREŽNÁ

Translated by Ruth Ahmedzai Kemp

Necklace/Choker

JANA BODNÁROVÁ

Translated by Jonathan Gresty

Vanity Unfair

ZUZANA CIGÁNOVÁ

Translated by Magdalena Mullek

MAREK VADAS

The Healer

and Other Stories

TRANSLATED BY
JULIA AND PETER SHERWOOD

LONDON CALCUTTA NEW YORK

Series Editor: JULIA SHERWOOD

This book has received a subsidy from SLOLIA Committee,
the Centre for Information on Literature in Bratislava, Slovakia.

Seagull Books, 2023

First published in Slovak as *Liečiteľ* by Koloman Kertész Bagala
© Marek Vadas, 2006

First published in English translation by Seagull Books, 2023
English translation © Julia Sherwood and Peter Sherwood, 2023

ISBN   978 1 80309 162 4

British Library Cataloguing-in-Publication Data
A catalogue record for this book is available from the British Library

Typeset by Seagull Books, Calcutta, India
Printed and bound by WordsWorth India, New Delhi, India

CONTENTS

THE HEALER

Ike felt he had finally turned a corner. He asked a street woodcarver to make him a round stamp with a lizard image that said 'Ike Ngoma—Soul Healer'. The words didn't have quite the right ring but in the heat of the day he couldn't think of anything better. Then he took a chicken and 300 francs to an official who dealt with all the paperwork without making too much fuss. Ike was now ready to launch his practice. People are always happy to reward those who get them out of trouble. They will bring you fruit, yams or sugar, even if they have nothing to eat themselves.

One morning Ike had gone to the market place as usual, and made eyes at a young seller until she treated him to a piece of fufu with meat sauce free of charge. Ike had been out of a job for nearly six months, ever since his boss sacked him from the warehouse. The boss claimed that some crates of Coca-Cola and beer had gone missing even though Ike was prepared to swear he'd never so much as blinked an eye when he was standing guard. And he was quite sure the owner had invented the missing goods just to get rid of him and give the job to some rascally relative of his who'd just turned up in town. But everything would be different now. He'd had a dream, which had given him a brilliant idea. In the dream he saw himself passing through a crowd of cripples. Their hands were clasped together in supplication and he healed them with a touch of his hand, by placing it on their brow, rubbing their temples, or gently touching their half-closed eyelids. People came to him with festering sores, with white larvae swarming inside cracks in their faces, men without noses, children with bloated bellies. People flocked to him in an endless procession—he couldn't even tell if they were walking or floating. They moved as if they were riding the escalator he'd seen a year back in a department store in Yaoundé. Rain streamed down their faces. It was raining so heavily that the earth became one with the sky. Red drops rose from the ground and vanished in the grey clouds. The eyes of the people in the crowd stared ahead into the middle distance, as if they had lost all hope and accepted their inevitable end. As he touched them mumbling a four-line chant an old man had taught him when he was still a boy, life would reignite in their glassy gaze and the blood would slowly drain from the whites of their eyes. Ike was sure that his dream gift would also work in real life. He knew because voices he trusted told him so.

He came to a bar and mingled with the customers until he found an unfinished beer bottle. He stood there sipping the beer slowly and watching the men play dice. Suddenly he could feel that someone had hit him on the head with a stick. His vision became blurred and the pain made him double up. When he recovered and turned around, he could see nothing suspicious behind him. In the street women balancing pots on their heads were slowly edging towards the market place and no one took any notice of him or of the people standing outside the bar. Ike rubbed the wound on the crown of his head and looked at the palm of his hand. It was covered in blood.

He went to the kitchen to rinse it off and tried to figure out what had happened. He wasn't sure if he was more angry or bewildered. He'd been in many fights as a teenager and often come home with bumps and grazes. But this pain was of a quite different order. There was something chilling about the blow.

Ike had bought spices and collected herbs, blended them together and packed them into small bottles he'd found on a rubbish dump behind a hotel. He numbered the bottles using his own system and divided them according to the source of the disease—mental and physical, the latter subdivided into external and internal.

Right at the beginning he was lucky to run into a few old women who were obviously in need of medicinal charcoal or herbs for dysentery. Any beginner could manage that after a few days' practice. Ike could additionally rely on the spell he'd learnt as a child, a few magic words that helped his practice get off to a smooth start. News of his triumphs spread fast, although he could boast of only a few successful cases. In a small town like Bamenda the word of an old woman is sacred.

His services soon earned Ike a carved chair that he placed next to his bed and he could buy a new pair of dancing sandals. He was able to swap some eggs for dried fish at the market and could afford beer without getting into debt. His life was on the up.

One day a desperate little shrivelled man came to his shack. He said Ike had to heal his sister. The girl was in hospital but the doctor didn't know what else he could do to help her. She'd had two operations already.

Ike went over to the hospital. There he found a pale young woman lying motionless with her eyes wide open, surrounded by gleaming, blood-red walls. The desperate man dragged him inside and he sat down face to face with the doctor.

The girl had been brought to the hospital screaming with pain. The doctor discovered it wasn't appendicitis but an advanced case of snail fever. They operated immediately and pulled out half a bucketful of threadworms. Her condition improved miraculously over a couple of weeks but just as she was about to leave the hospital, her legs gave way and her pulse all but disappeared. The doctors came running in and when they cut her belly open they found her bowels were again swarming with thin worms about 20 centimetres long. They removed over five kilos of them. Since then the girl had been in agony and the doctor couldn't think of anything more he could do, other than morphine injections.

Ike reeled back and went out into the fresh air. It was noon and sweat stung his eyes. He was gasping at the mere idea of this case. He wanted to go back to the wretched man and apologize. But as he took a few steps and was about to enter the hospital, he was struck by another blunt blow to his head. This one was much more powerful than the first, and Ike fainted and collapsed.

The dark fog before him parted and a huge black bird appeared. It landed on his belly and scanned Ike's face with its enormous eyes. It was the doctor who'd carried Ike back to the hospital to treat his wound. Still lying in bed, Ike propped himself up on his elbows and saw an invisible man sitting next to the doctor and the desperate little shrivelled man. The invisible man's legs dangled from the bed and he played with a long stick that looked like a hoe handle, watching Ike intently as he regained consciousness. Then he gestured to indicate that he was there incognito. He was invisible to the doctor and the other man; Ike was the only one who could see him.

Later that day the invisible man came to his house and casually apologized for the blow, admitting he'd rather overdone it. He walked around the hut, swinging his stick all the time and tapping the furniture, the bed and the damp paperboard walls. Sometimes he would frown, then give an appreciative nod and mumble something under his breath as if appraising a property he was planning to buy.

Although he spoke to Ike in a friendly tone, calling him 'my dear friend', he didn't appear to be kind. Ike didn't like his piercing, cadaverous eyes or the tone of his voice as, instead of ordering him to do something, he'd say something softly along the lines of 'no doubt you will agree', or 'you know very well that this will be best for you', or 'I'm sure you won't say no'. Ike listened to him as if bewitched and unable to resist and agreed he would go on treating the girl whom the whole hospital had written off. The invisible man promised to be on hand and to help if need be. As he had done before, unbeknownst to Ike.

The visitor stayed until dinnertime. They shared a meal of fufu with fish sauce, washing it down with home-brewed beer from a stall across the street. Then the invisible man waved his stick by way of goodbye and vanished into the darkness.

When the door slammed behind him, Ike was relieved. He felt as if all day long his body had done nothing but do the bidding of the man with the stick. Only now did he realize that the man had him completely under his spell. He wondered what to do in this situation. He checked his supplies of herbs and kept reciting the childhood spell over and over again. He dressed his wound, stretched out on the mattress and closed his eyes.

He dreamt of the girl in the hospital. Her body was swathed in enormous worms. The worms dragged her towards a foaming brown river. She tried to hold on to sharp rocks that stuck out from the roadside but the worms kept biting her hand. The clumps of grass that her fingers grasped slithered easily out of the soil of their own accord. Ike stood on the riverbank with wild beasts and other creatures, watching her hopeless struggle. His legs were made of stone and his tongue had turned to wood. Before he could reach out to her the worms had dragged her under the water for good.

He woke up gasping for air and drenched in sweat. A night storm was raging outside and the air in the shack was heavy and musty, as if someone had scattered corpses all over the place. His head wound under the bandage was still festering and the pain would not subside, not even special bandages helped. Ike screamed the most horrible curses he could think of out into the roaring thunder. He was gripped by impotent fury at the invisible man who'd punished him for no reason, all the while pretending to help him. Ike had sacrificed all his strength to heal the sick only to be dealt a blow from which he couldn't recover. He ran out into the rain and started to walk down the long street towards the market place. He didn't know why but he felt compelled to leave his house whose walls were pressing down on him, making him feel ever smaller.

A lone lantern flickered in the wind in the middle of the square. In the flooded road the potholes in the tarmac filled with water. Ike stepped into several potholes and hurt his ankles because he'd just put on his dancing sandals as he ran out of the house. When he half-closed his eyes the streams of rainwater merged into a dark pane of glass. From behind this he could vaguely make out the outlines of figures from the first, old dream in which he had seen himself as a healer. He saw the old women suffering from diarrhoea, the leprous children with severed limbs, the desperate shrivelled little man, and a herb seller from the market. Some nodded a greeting while others stood still, the whites of their eyes shining and motionless in the darkness.

He didn't know how he ended up in front of the hospital building. The sound of rain drumming on the tin roof was deafening and the slight flame from an impromptu campfire glowed in the corridor. The invisible man emerged out of the dusk and led him towards the girl. She was lying on the floor next to the fire. Ike realized that the rain was coming down in torrents under the roof, just like outside. He knelt down in a puddle, mechanically following the invisible man's orders. He rubbed some oil into the girl's damp belly, quietly repeating the magic spell from his dream over and over again. He heard monotonous voices reciting incomprehensible prayers behind his back. He felt weaker and weaker and didn't even notice that blood from his head wound began to drip onto the girl's shiny skin. The blood mingled with the oil and he went on rubbing it more and more slowly. His vision clouded over and for a moment he thought he saw what appeared to be black strings before his eyes.

The worms slowly began to wind around Ike's hands. Soon he was unable to remove them. He was kneeling above the lifeless body of the girl in the middle of a small clearing in the woods out of town. All he could see was the smouldering fire. Then the hand of the invisible man gently touched his forehead. He was overcome by faintness, then burning heat. He collapsed head first onto the woman's bare breasts.

As his body shuddered in its death throes he tried to summon all his remaining strength to mouth a sentence. His lips formed the spell that had helped him so many times before, taught to him by someone in the forest when he was a little boy:

> *You who have no body*
> *I beg you: let me feel no pain.*
> *You who take the dead*
> *I beg you: let me wake again.*

VISIT TO LAMBARÉNÉ

After crossing the Gulf of Guinea by plane, I continued some 60 miles upstream through the murky waters of the Ogooué River. Here I was in Gabon, at the Schweitzer Infirmary in Lambaréné, standing in front of an old wooden cross overgrown with weeds, bearing the name of the mustachioed *grand docteur* Albert Schweitzer. A few bandaged amputees were out for their morning walk. I was on a highly confidential mission to find out more about a mysterious herb once used there to treat alcoholism. To be honest, I was in desperate need of that wretched weed myself.

I walked around the museum trying to win over the tour guide in a white lab coat with small talk as I looked at old photographs and manuscripts in the glass display cases. There weren't as many as I had expected, and they weren't what I had hoped to see. In fact, I wasn't really sure what exactly I was looking for. All I could see were copies of immunization records, extracts from *The Philosophy of Civilization* and Bach oratorios by the dozen. Most of the exhibits were of no use to me—surgical instruments, Schweitzer's clothes and his pedal piano. In another section there was even a stand offering a bizarre assortment of traditional musical instruments and paintings made by the hospital's patients. One oil painting depicted a body drowning in a tropical forest swamp; it was in its final agony, just one hand still sticking out above its surface, and some incensed spirits hovering above it in the air. The artist was buried nearby.

'Where do you keep all of your medical histories, the lists of patients with their medication dosages and descriptions of the traditional herbs the doctor used? Surely they haven't all been taken back to Europe?'

'No, they hadn't.' The guide chuckled. 'Some of them had rotted away, others had been lost, and the rest are in the Mission safe.' 'Could I take a look?' Of course I couldn't.

Nor was she keen to have her picture taken with a drum. 'No snap!' Let alone anything else . . .

I set off in search of a bar. In fact, every building around the place was a bar. Wherever you spotted a banner with the logo of a brewery, you could get warm beer for 400 francs. I walked into the first shack. There was a blind old man sitting inside. As soon as I said hello, he pointed to a crate in the corner. I thanked him, helped myself to a couple of bottles, and put them on the table. I started to explain what I was looking for, but he interrupted me before I could finish my first sentence. He already knew. But he had to disappoint me—I wasn't going to find anything. There was nothing of the kind at the museum, and it was quite a few years since the last healer had died. But I could try to follow the healer to the afterworld and ask my question.

We had another beer. The old man told me that it was quite easy to enter the spirit world. I'd have to pass a food shack, head for the woods, and after about a mile I'd see a clearing. There would be a tall palm tree growing just beyond it. I'd have to climb to the top, and there I'd find the entrance. But I wouldn't be able to enter as I was. The spirits didn't like White men roaming about in their world. I'd first have to go to a bar and find some local guy who'd be willing to swap bodies with me for a day. The old man would have been happy to give me his own, but he was blind, so it would have been of no use. I borrowed his juju and left.

As it happened, I wasn't able to ask any questions in the Lambaréné afterworld. The local spirits didn't look upon me with favour. They were a weird bunch, more keen on mocking me and not at all interested in sharing their secrets. I asked. 'Where is Petit Manu? I just want to ask him for one particular herb, then I'll be gone, like my thirst for beer.' They looked down on me even though I was disguised as a Black rubber gatherer with the flattest of noses and my left arm hacked off, supposedly after an attack by a leopard. The spirits didn't give a damn about my problems, and one of them even told me to beat it and flung an old skull at me with all his might. So I had to return from the tropical forest none the wiser and climb down the tallest palm tree, back to the warmth of the sodden soil and the mortal creatures.

But where was my friend, the guy from the bar who'd agreed to a body swap after 10 beers?

I spotted him later that night. Actually, I spotted myself outside a bar in the square, carrying a big bottle of Guinness and his (that is, my) hair all mussed up, surrounded by a bunch of drunken patients. He was spewing nonsense, of course, and you could hear him two streets away. He said he lived in Europe, on the seventieth floor of a skyscraper. The people of this town, which boasted only three buildings two storeys high, were so impressed that they bought him another beer. And he'd managed to rip my pants, spill beer all over my shirt, and get my chin drenched in blood.

When he saw me from the corner of his eye, he pretended he'd never met me and kept blathering on. That rattled me. I elbowed my way through the crowd towards him, grabbed the grease-stained shirt of mine around his neck and hissed into his ear that he should step out for a word. He looked frightened and howled for people to get me off him, claiming I was a sorcerer about to steal his soul. Someone else in the crowd yelled that he'd heard me asking for his body. The passers-by jumped on me, jostling and hitting me; someone even bit me on the neck. I had no choice but to beat a retreat. It was hard to defend myself, outnumbered as I was and with only one arm. I had no choice: as this couldn't be settled amicably, I had to reach into my pocket and use the blind man's juju.

Everyone froze in horror. I went up to the Black bastard who'd pretended to be my friend in the bar but was in fact only looking for an easy and dishonest way to get hold of a healthy body, leaving me stuck as a cripple forever. I gazed into his eyes and at their core I saw his soul, gleaming, slightly drunk, horrified and duplicitous . . .

I grabbed his soul firmly with one hand and wrenched it out of my original White body until his irises went dark. When I dragged it out into the sunlight and threw it to the ground, the soul gave a frightened shriek and scurried off to hide behind the nearest villager, who stood frozen like a statue. The soul glowered at me from behind him, frightened.

I entered my own body and turned into myself again. The hollow frame of the one-armed Black man who pretended to be my friend for a moment collapsed onto the ground like an old diving suit. After briefly savouring the anxiety of his soul I let it return to where it belonged. Humbled, it scampered back, head bowed low, and climbed inside. As soon as the guy straightened up, the villagers awoke from their torpor and angrily chased him into the woods.

Good job I had the juju on me, or I would never have managed to pull this off! All that was left to do was wash my clothes. I just hoped they weren't covered in puke . . .

I went back to the blind man, ready to tell him what had happened in the afterworld. But he didn't need me to tell him anything. He already knew I hadn't fared well. It would have been far too easy. He wished me luck.

It's tough being an alcoholic.

YELLOW EYES

The stars are out above the town. A White man stands by the swimming pool of the staff hotel. He looks down absent-mindedly at the guard dog rubbing itself against his feet. The dog reeks of rubbish he rummages through when its master helps to unload deliveries at the reception or sings in church.

The dog's eyes are aglow in the dark. One of its ears is folded back and flies are teeming around a festering wound. A memento of a fight with a rat. The White man absentmindedly pats the dog on its mangy fur. The dog growls with delight and bounds towards the gate, barking, to show off. Meanwhile the man dives into the pool. Even though the water is warm, it's refreshing to feel the moisture caressing his body. He dives under. He sees a pair of eyes below the surface. The shining yellow eyes draw his gaze, luring him to come closer. He swims further down in pursuit. The eyes are getting ever closer in a hypnotic whirl. The veins on his temples bulge, he exhales a little. A few bubbles rise to the surface. The eyes grow larger, spinning faster and faster.

The White man is aware he ought to rise to the surface and fill his lungs with air but instead he grabs hold of the pipe feeding the pool. Only when he comes so close to the whirling eyes that they are level with his own does he strain every muscle to propel himself upwards. But one hand gets stuck in a cranny behind the pipe. Confused, he writhes about and breathes in some water. The eyes disappear and everything goes blank.

The man's wrists and ankles are handcuffed below the surface of the water. A sudden nervous burst propels him to make a final attempt. His face breaks through the black surface into the light.

He is lying in the courtyard under a lamp. Around him squat black faces—two waiters and a security guard from the reception. The dog that had been scared of water all its life had saved his. It dived below him and carried him to the surface on his back. The White man recovers and glances at his saviour. It is lying in the grass, still panting, its paw scratching a wounded ear irritated by the chlorine in the swimming pool.

The White man is sitting in a small bar opposite the hotel garage. He's drinking chilled beer with chunks of ice floating in it. The yellow eyes he saw in the swimming pool have never stopped haunting him. They visit him in his dreams in the form of eyes of animals roaming the streets and in daytime splinters of rocks glittering after rain bring back the memory of the eyes. They appear to him in the faces of stallholders. They gaze out at him from the clear night sky.

Each encounter with the eyes leaves him more and more frightened, the whirling circles assail him with increasing urgency and intensity. His heart is thumping louder and louder.

He is sitting in a bar outside the hotel entrance. The dog runs out of the gate as a van comes hurtling down the street. It manages to honk but doesn't slow down or swerve, not even an inch. The round headlights flare up in the dusk and devour the dog.

The White man gets up. He knocks the table with his knee, spilling his own and his companion's beer. He goes up to the motionless, headless animal body. The van disappears in traffic at the far end of the crossroads. He sees the headlights again as they approach his startled face. The huge, gleaming yellow eyes that carry him into the dark.

He sits down in the dust of the road and throws up. He feels nothing.

THE SCHEMER

The folks living in our small town are the loveliest people on earth. As you walk to work in the morning it's quite common to come across a bloodied corpse lying on the pavement, a memento of a turbulent night when the evil spirit Imbu the Schemer had crept into someone's head.

Whenever that happens, a man prompted by the Schemer will get hold of a knife or, out of the blue, start punching a neighbour's head or, more often, the head of someone sitting at the next table in a bar. It usually happens in a bar, because this evil spirit likes to hang around watering holes where men drink lots of beer and palm wine. Come evening, Imbu wanders around the tables where drink has been spilt, and while the people sitting there can't see him, he can certainly see them, as he bends over the glasses and overturned bottles to stare them in the eye. And if he should find someone with bulging veins and glassy eyes, he will try to get into that man's body. Or, sometimes, a woman's. Imbu looks around and cautiously begins to probe the thoughts in his target's mind, even prodding their memory to ensure that their protective spirit is fast asleep, dulled by the beer they had drunk. Then he addresses his target in the familiar voice of his protective spirit. He slips all sorts of ideas into his head, for example that the fellow across the table, who is surely rolling in money, let someone buy him a drink but won't buy a round himself, that he's a bastard who's been giving his wife sleazy looks and, to add insult to injury, has mocked him for being out of a job. Once Imbu sees that his talk is beginning to have an effect, he lets up somewhat and prompts the man to buy another drink to forget his problems and the wicked world. A man in this state looks around in a haze, his head slumped to one side, then goes to buy another drink feeling so miserable that his eyelids droop and the figures dancing around him are just a blur. By now the evil spirit is comfortably ensconced inside him, waiting for his moment. Sometimes the man he has sneaked into will give a shudder, wriggle about on his chair and pretend not to give a damn about anything, with only a leg nervously jiggling up and down under the table. When the right moment comes, Imbu makes the man turn around just as the bastard, who won't buy anyone a drink and keeps mocking him, has asked his wife or daughter to dance and starts rubbing himself against her without shame or fear. At this point he breaks out of his seeming lethargy; his shuddering muscles turn to stone and he leaps at his new rival with a howl. His fist lands on the other man's face so hard that you can hear the bones crack, and the lecher falls on the ground. He gets up because, of course, he can't let our man get away with it, and the two charge at each other with hands, knives, wooden boards and bottles. The bar owner starts shrieking, the other customers try to pull them apart, but back away once they also get hit. They form a circle around the men fighting and watch from a safe distance. Before long one of the men ends up lying lifeless in the mud by the gutter and everyone scatters to the winds. It's closing time.

Next morning the bartenders peer at the corpse through the gaps in the shutters and mothers grab hold of their children's T-shirts to stop them running out into the street and being confronted with death. But the children do catch sight of it, for children see more than adults will admit. Sometimes it takes a couple of days before the bartenders come to an agreement and collect enough money to bribe a policeman, who will arrange for the corpse to be taken away.

FLYING WOMEN

A small group of women gathered around the well in the middle of the square, folded up some pieces of fabric, put them on their heads and lifted vessels filled with water onto them. The younger ones kept giggling while the others carried their load with a vacant stare. They swayed to and fro and wiggled their bottoms, their skirts aflutter as if sending a message to days gone by.

Sometimes a bird would alight on the vessels on top of their heads and take a sip of water. The women cast shadows on the ground like impassive statues that ruffle up the plumage on their heads every now and then, before spreading out their wings ready to fly. Then they fold away their wings again and continue to carry their load all the way home without ever taking flight. They never take off, not even for a second.

THERE'S NOTHING
FOR ME TO FORGET

'Where were you again last night?' his wife asked brusquely in the morning as she banged a plate down on the table in front of him.

Where had he been all night? Good question! At around nine he was at the Horse Bar—after that it's a total blank. All he knows is that he must have gone to eat somewhere because he doesn't find the steaming chicken feet tempting at all. Normally he'd give anything for a chance to wolf them down but now the mere sight of them makes his stomach heave. And this is not the first time he's been unable to answer this kind of question from his wife.

He's been forgetting things more and more often lately. He can't recall what he did at night, at work he can't remember whether he's been home and in the evening he has no idea what he's been up to all day long.

Where were you all night? That might be a good question to ask someone who frequents bars with his workmates, who chases the cheap prostitutes by the railway station or on the outskirts, or keeps a mistress. But none of the above applies to him. He just comes home, and the minute he takes off his shoes, he is startled by this question. How would you respond in his place?

I've just been out with my friends.

I can't for the life of me remember a single moment of last night.

I fell asleep at my desk at work. I've been so busy lately.

I went to eye up the young girls.

He could say the first thing that springs to mind, he could look for excuses, or rack his brain for the most plausible guess. But none of these would be the truth.

There's a void in his head—like all the days that drag on one after the other, all the nights that leave no memory.

'I didn't go anywhere and didn't do anything. Believe me. I tell you no lie.'

THE KING IS WAITING

They travelled light as they knew they couldn't manage the long journey with a big load. And besides, they're not women to be carrying loads! Although they never talked about it, they both had great admiration for their mother, who was able to lug a huge gas canister on her head all the way from the market while also holding a basketful of cassava tubers on her back. Women have the stamina for it, as the boys discovered when they were supposed to bring a gas canister to a warehouse and the two of them together couldn't shift it. Men have other things to do. Chop down a palm tree during wine harvest time, build huts, keep peace in the house, that sort of thing.

They won't need much on the journey as most of it will be on their territory. Every Eton will offer them food and a bed for the night free of charge, especially as they are the sons of the king. They are taking the news of their father's death to their eldest brother so he can succeed him on the Man-el-lone throne. Their brother Ndoua is already 18 and studying forestry in Dschang. Their father's dying wish was for his firstborn to bury him. Otherwise he would never find peace.

In every Eton village they were welcomed with open arms. They were directed to the village elder and offered cola nuts and fresh black pepper and salt. They drank a small barrel of palm wine, shared the latest news from their neighbourhood and received valuable advice for their journey. The village elder's wife gave them cassava and a bag of ground nuts, or whatever treat she happened to have at hand.

The humid season arrived earlier than usual, making their journey more arduous. It took them three days to reach the end of their territory. When they set off on their journey, no one in their village had any idea of the distance to the town where their brother lived. They knew only that it lay somewhere beyond the last Eton village. They would just have to ask around, find their brother and return with him as soon as possible.

The fertile valleys dotted with small settlements disappeared, giving way to a dense forest full of nighttime perils. They knew the woods around their native village like the back of their hand. They knew exactly which paths to avoid and even blindfold could find the trees that were useful—those that bore the finest fruit or yielded wine or acted as the guardians of order. Man-e-lone was famous for a palm that was eternally ablaze. A long time ago, the tree, almost 20 metres high, was struck by lightning and set ablaze. Next morning, after the storm blew over, the crown of the tree was still on fire. Any other tree would have been destroyed by the fire by then but this one kept burning steadily for a very long time. At first, the villagers were scared that the fire would spread to their fields but the flames gradually steadied, billowing gently in the wind. People would gaze at the canopy every night as the tree turned into a blazing torch. Gradually they stopped being afraid and came to treat it as a kind of natural lighthouse which showed the way to travellers descending the hills from the direction of Monatélé.

But one evening a fragment from the tree's canopy broke loose. The wind carried the burning piece a great distance, all the way to Mevo's hut. Mevo was a strange man, a loner. It set his house on fire straight away and it burned to ashes within the hour. Poor Mevo barely managed to escape, with his eight goats. He ran to the king, trembling all over and begging for mercy. He confessed that he had cast a spell on the market traders from the village and that was why they couldn't sell their harvest of ground nuts and tomatoes. Even if they managed to sell some, the money in their pockets would turn into worthless scraps of paper. What made Mevo confess was that he'd heard a voice just before the red-hot embers fell onto his straw roof. The voice that sounded like the king's uttered a warning. It said that the fire from the palm tree was punishment for his black magic. To atone for his deeds, he showed the village folk how to protect themselves from this kind of spell. All they had to do was place at the bottom of a basket a small fruit that grew on the bushes by the stream. From then on the villagers no longer had any trouble at the market. Quite the contrary—people in Centre Ville and Monatélé could hardly wait for the famous tomatoes from Man-e-lone.

The story of the voice and the scorched hut bolstered the palm tree's extraordinary fame. It kept watch over the life in the village from its fiery crown, always on the alert for anyone with ill intentions. The brothers learnt this from their father. His words were corroborated by others who added juicy details about other incidents when the tree had intervened. The brothers were aware of what the forest and the spirits hidden in the trees were capable of. That was why they were particularly in awe when they entered a thicket no one else from their tribe had explored before. Except for their much older brother. Or maybe not even he, since he had been driven to the distant city that shines bright even at night in a foreign-made ministerial car.

The thick forest and darkness were not the only things the brothers feared. They also grew anxious because the journey was taking much longer than they had anticipated. A week had passed and still no one they asked knew anything about the north-western province or the city of Dschang. And they were afraid of their father's wrath, certain that he followed their movements as he should have been buried a long time ago.

They had to press ahead travelling by night as well as by day. They would take an hour's nap before sunset, then share some cola nuts and set off, chewing as they walked. With every fresh gust of wind strange faces emerged from the crowns of the trees. Some stared at them vaguely and in silence, others opened their fearsome mouths allowing the ancestors from the land of the dead to speak through them. They chided the brothers for not making enough headway and preferring their own comfort to the dying wishes of their father and king.

'Your father is waiting for you and he's not best pleased,' rustled the leaves on the mango trees. 'The king is angry,' the dry leaves of the breadfruit concurred and their moans mingled with the wailing of evil spirits.

The boys pressed their hands to their ears and ran into the darkness. After a few metres they ended up on the ground. They hunkered down by the trunk of a palm tree. The voices faded away. They wanted to look around but the moon had waned and they couldn't see anything in the dark. An invisible hand shut their eyes.

The next morning they were woken early by birdsong and a fresh surge of energy. They flew through forests, stopping at the markets only long enough to have a quick bite of cassava. Eventually they reached Kumbo, a beautiful town dotted with palaces and surrounded by red hills. They headed straight for the local shaman and asked for his help.

'Our father can wait no longer. We should have brought our brother home by now. We've done our best but we're worried that if we don't keep our promise, we shall never be able to go back,' they said to the old man. They paid him 500 francs and a few shells from the River Sanga on top. He said they should head for Mount Oku, climb up to the crater at the top of the hill and make a sacrifice of cola nuts and palm wine at the magic lake that was home to good spirits. They were sure to know their father and would help them.

But finding some palm wine in the mountains at this time of the year proved difficult. They asked at several bars but were met with laughter. Only in the last bar on the outskirts of Kumbo they managed to find a few drops of imported mimbo at the bottom of a barrel. But the wine was overripe, cloudy and foul smelling. 'I wonder if the spirits will like it,' the older brother said doubt-fully and gave a shudder after tasting it. He was used to the very best mimbo and being able to choose it at several different stages of fermentation. Nevertheless, they filled a bottle and set off. They didn't reach the foot of Mount Oku until the evening.

Just as they settled down to sleep, they felt drops of a sweet liquid on their forehead. Wine was dripping from the palm tree above them. They turned their mouths to the sky and quickly concluded that the only thing this taste resembled was their homegrown wine. This was the Man-e-Lone mimbo, from the palm their father had planted next to his house after the birth of his eldest son. They could not mistake this wine for anything else in the world. They drank some of the mimbo that dripped from above and spoke to them in their native tongue. It provided the best possible protection in this unfamiliar world. The brothers fell asleep hugging the tree trunk, the cockles of their hearts warmed by the taste of home.

When they woke up, there was no trace of the palm tree. All that was left was the taste of the wine on their palates and a small jar of white liquid fermented to perfection. They were certain that it was their palm that had come to their rescue. The unique taste of its wine and the characteristic notches on the trunk were clear proof of it. Had anyone tried to convince them that trees can't walk, they wouldn't have believed. Every child in their village knew that trees could watch people, follow in their footsteps at night, keep them company and show them the way if they got lost, but could also haunt them in their sleep. The brothers knew what trees were capable of.

They had once seen with their very own eyes a palm tree kill an evil White man who had stolen land from the people of Man-e-lone. He had ordered some trees in the bush to be chopped down so he could mine precious stones and build roads. And the palm tree killed him, taking matters into its own hands. It fell on the side exactly opposite to where everyone expected it to fall. It hit the hillside, right where the White man was standing. Giuseppe was his name. His body was flattened into the ground. Everyone in the village could point out the spot. Some said it was the work of a shaman. Others claimed that the trunk of the palm was home to the soul of an elder who could no longer bear to see the trees being felled. Be that as it may, the tree trunk landed in the least likely spot.

The boys threw away the bottle with the disgusting fake from Kumbo that might have offended the spirits. They climbed up to the crater and offered up a sacrifice of the wine on the shore of the lake, just as the shaman told them to.

After descending from the mountain they headed west. They passed several tradespeople with handcarts and decided to ask if this was the right way to Dschang and how far they still had to go.

But the traders took no notice of them. They all stood there as if turned to stone. They were like statues that would not come to life. Soon the brothers discovered that not only the tradespeople but the whole of nature appeared to be frozen that day. Leaves on trees didn't move and birds hung suspended in the sky in mid-flight. Time had stopped.

They were baffled for a moment but then realized it was their prayers that had brought the world to a standstill. They passed briskly through villages now packed ever closer to one another. They had no idea how long they spent walking like this before they at last reached the outskirts of Dschang. They had never before seen such an enormous city and such big crowds heading for the city centre. They lost their way among the throng of stall-holders, their stalls piled high with fabrics and enticing wares of a kind that had never made it to their village. They battled their way through a herd of unmoving goats and taciturn food sellers. All they needed to do was reach out and pick up a roasted corn on the cob or some of the juiciest pieces of meat from the spits.

No one would have seen them, no stallholder could have chased after them.

After searching high and low they finally reached the college where their brother Ndoua was a student. They found him frozen in a strange posture in front of his room. But as soon as they shook him, he came to, unlike the people they had passed on the road. The news of their father's death came as a big blow to him, even though he had had a premonition. For several days now unusual omens had been alarming him.

The return journey passed much more quickly. And as soon as they set foot on Eton territory, the world came back to life. Hens started clucking and people resumed their activities as if nothing had happened. Their father was laid out on the ceremonial bed. Despite the magic of Oku Mountain, more than a week had passed since he died, yet his body showed no sign of decay. It was as if he had died just moments earlier. He was delighted to see his eldest son by his side. Ndoua could now take over his duties and he could depart in peace. He could rest in the red mud which makes trees and flowers grow. He said goodbye to his fields, his hut and his loyal people. He had been waiting a long time for this moment. And he was happy to embark on this journey in the company of his eldest son.

He lay down in his grave, settled into a comfortable position and allowed himself to be covered with soil. The brothers marked the spot with stones and a bottle of palm wine which they came to replace regularly. Soon a hibiscus with fragrant red blossoms began to grow next to it. The villagers knew that it was through these flowers that their king kept eyes on their world.

HOTEL BEAU REGARD

He stepped on a cockroach. Lately there have been more of them than strictly necessary. Especially up here, on the first floor: you can barely get into the bathroom. They used to be quite rare, never larger than an ordinary matchstick. Nowadays it's quite common to come across a big fat specimen with a body larger than a good-sized thumb and feelers just as long. It's high time he got hold of some lime or that disgusting chemical stuff at the shops. A cockroach infestation of this kind is hardly good for a hotel's reputation. People don't like them. And besides, the roaches gobble up food, old wallpaper and before you know it they'll even have a go at the furniture.

He went out onto the terrace, rolled himself a cigarette, took a long drag and leaned on the railing. He watched the people returning from work, keeping an eye out for anyone he knew, who might stop for a quick chat. He's been managing the hotel on the square all on his own for quite a few years now. He sweeps the corridors, fixes whatever needs fixing and deals with all the paperwork. He hangs around the coach station waiting for new arrivals who might be looking for accommodation. 'Hotel Beau Regard! Large rooms with a fan! Lockable doors! Come and have a look, we offer the best views in town! Hotel Beau Regard! At a friendly price!' he shouts as he darts among the vehicles.

Passengers covered in dust and sweat get off the bus stiff and shaken up, and wait for their luggage to be unloaded. No one is interested in a hotel room. Everyone is trying to save money and besides, there's no reason why they should go to a hotel. They have relatives here, or they have come only for the market. To buy and sell before returning to their home town in the evening—they hail a cab and are gone. There are many more people here now than back in the day, when his father opened the hotel. But business has been going downhill.

Come evening he's back on the terrace where there was once a well-known bar where people came to drink and dance. Beer was guzzled by the gallon, men would sit around drinking and drumming till late into the night, older women would gossip at the back and younger ones would just hang around outside, preening themselves before the men. He would serve drinks and dance attendance on the customers, sweeping the gnawed bones off the tables and sometimes, with serving tray in hand, he'd join the dancers as they swayed to the rhythm of the makossa. He'd shake his hips and sing along with his favourite chorus:

If my wife leaves me, no problem.
If she cheats on me, no problem.
If I lose my job, no problem.
If I'm broke, no problem.
No problem, no problem.

In those days he was the most quick-witted of singers, second to none when it came to adding ever more lines to the chorus. He can still replay it in his mind's eye as if it were yesterday. Friends would give him good-humoured thumps on the back and a tip big enough for a bottle of chilled beer.

He puts out his cigarette and goes back to check the rooms. The electricity is down again, the whole town centre is without power. The light of the candles sends the insects scurrying into the corners of the room. There are so many cockroaches here that they crackle under the soles of his shoes. He tightens the taps just in case, even though no water has flowed out of them this year. He blows out the candle and stretches out on a bed in one of the rooms.

In the morning he starts a fire and warms up yesterday's pap. Who knows, maybe he'll have some guests today?

He has filled his plate but hasn't touched the food. He just likes the smell of the pap, suffused with hot chillies. He wonders if he should invite some politician to his hotel. Or a football player. He could throw a party for them, that should pull in the crowds. If his place is good enough for a football player, why shouldn't it be good enough for ordinary folk? Then he'll give them a tour of the rooms so they can see for themselves. He may not be able to offer the luxury of the hotels in the capital, but all the basics are here.

His musings are interrupted by the sound of an engine outside the entrance. A bang of the door, the sound of footsteps. The creaking of door hinges. He leaps out of the armchair and rushes over to the bar. Men in overalls and helmets are milling about. A White man stands in the doorway and surveys the place.

'What can I get you?' he says, his eyes agleam. This is the first time a White man has set foot in his place!

But the men pay him no attention. They pick up chairs, open windows, tap on walls and examine the ceiling, as if looking for holes through which water might leak during a thunderstorm.

'Good morning, gentlemen! How can I help you?' he repeats.

Today is his lucky day. How many times has he dreamt of playing host to White people. His father had never set eyes on a White man, but when he handed the hotel over to him, he stressed that he should always be obliging to them. You never know what you might need later. He is so excited he's at a loss as to how to welcome them as warmly as possible. He just stands there helplessly, watching them march past him.

'There's beer, palm wine, real matango, there's also mimbo from the coast. Fufu, mackerel and vegetable pap. Everything first class,' he says, pacing up and down the room. First in order to get into the White men's field of vision, then to jump out of their way. There's something strange about these guests! They are gazing at a point somewhere behind him and not only are they not responding, but they aren't even taking any notice of him.

Meanwhile one of the men goes behind the bar and pushes at the counter. He has no difficulty yanking it out at the first attempt. He hurls the counter out of the window, followed by three of his best chairs.

'But, but . . . you can't do that!' he screams, stunned. 'Who do you think you are?!'

But the men take no notice of him, and their White boss keeps staring at some papers in his hand. He folds them up and says, 'Everything's fine.' They can go ahead. The place will be demolished by the evening.

'Are you out of your mind? Don't you dare! This is my hotel!' he yells, throwing the kerosene lamp on the floor in fury.

The men by the exit come to a halt. 'Did you hear that?' says one, staring into the room intently. 'Sounded like a bang . . . I don't like places like this.'

The other man smiles and pats him on the shoulder. Λ moment later the bulldozer's engine starts up.

BROWN ONE DAY,
BLACK THE NEXT

I know what women are like! They have but one thing on their minds: how to catch a man. I'm 35 and have met more than one witch of the kind. But I've always managed to resist their witchcraft. And believe me, sometimes it's no mean task to get away from a female and save your skin. But I am Bassa and I won't let anyone try their tricks on me! My father worked for many years as an assistant for Ayissi, the most famous marabout far and wide. He told me so many stories that they would last me to my dying day. I have a pretty good understanding of what to watch out for when I'm dealing with women and all that they're capable of.

Say you're in a bar and order a beer. If you let your guard down for even a second, a woman will slip a strand of her hair into your beer. You take a sip and you're done for. You'll never look at another woman again, except for that bitch. It's a tried and tested trick, but it's old and trite and only works with careless fools. Whenever I order a beer, I make sure I open the can myself, obviously, and I don't let it out of my sight for a second.

My father told me how one of these witches tricked his friend Faustin, an educated man who had studied in the capital. He caught her eye at a New Year's party. All he wanted was to have some palm wine and a dance but she kept joining him at his table, rubbing herself against his hips while they danced, making him buy her drinks. They downed a few together and Faustin swore that nothing else happened. While they danced, she contrived to pluck out a strand of his hair and then went to see a shaman. She gave him Faustin's hair along with a dead man's tooth as well as 10 eggs, a glob of her morning spit and a 1,000 francs. After the party, Faustin forgot all about the witch but sometime later she appeared to him in a dream. She cooked dinner for him and slept with him.

The dream was visceral, and when Faustin woke up the next morning he noticed that his belly was full, as if he'd a real meal and made love to her. He never saw the woman again but from that night onwards he kept searching for her desperately, and his yearning was so strong that he went out of his mind. That is why you must be wary even while dreaming, should a pretty woman's face appear to you. And if a beautiful woman offers you some food in your sleep—refuse it, come what may.

Something similar has happened to me too but it wasn't a dream, and fortunately it all turned out well—I was well prepared for this sort of thing. I had some errands to run in Akolingue, a small town by Lake Nyong. When my father heard where I was headed, he spent the whole night before my departure dispensing useful advice. He told me stories of a black lake you must keep away from as it will swallow you up before you even dip your toe in the water. He also described all kinds of tricks the local womenfolk use to cast a spell on men. The women from around Lake Yong are the most dangerous of shrews and in their presence you should never, not for a moment, drop your guard . . . No boozing in bars—that's just what they're waiting for. For drink makes you vulnerable and foolish.

My journey through the mud-caked roads was long and arduous. Held up by lorries axle-deep in sludge, I didn't reach Akonaligue until late at night, tired, thirsty and hungry. I walked into the nearest restaurant, a half-empty shack by the station, took a seat and ordered a beer. I was served by a strikingly beautiful and suspicious-looking barmaid who suggested I order roast kanga. Kanga, the best fish in the world, which the locals catch in the black lake. I knew at once what lay behind the offer! My father had told me all about it. I politely refused and went in search of a meal elsewhere.

I walked along the high street lined with noisy dives but none had any decent food on offer. Right at the end, close to a roundabout, I found a cosy little bar. A few couples were quietly sipping their beer, and I ordered one myself. Here too, the only food on the menu was kanga. I was too tired to traipse all the way to the centre of town and keep scouring the side streets, it was almost midnight. The woman at the fish kiosk looked rather agreeable and didn't seem at all suspect. So I ordered kanga despite my wariness. I knew that in order to keep out of harm's way I had to have my wits about me and follow my father's advice. Kanga is a rare fish with the most delicate flesh. However, it is used in magic more often than is any other fish. The head is the tastiest part—a treat no man will forego—and women, aware of this, hide their juju in it. Once you've eaten a kanga head you will forget everything, all your obligations, your wife, your children. You will live only for the woman who prepared the fish for you. That's why you must never eat kanga alone—make the woman join you at the table and eat with you, or ask some friends to join you, or find an excuse. While I waited for the fish to be brought over by

Desirée (that was the name of the woman behind the bar), I ordered a pitcher of water. I waited to see what she would do but she brought the water without the slightest hesitation. That was a good sign—water is a very potent medicine, and before eating kanga you have to drink at least one glassful.

Gradually, my misgivings melted away. I drank some water and from where I sat I had a good view of the cook and the grill where she was roasting the fish. I was not in danger because I had a few more precautions up my sleeve. Keeping an eye on Desirée, I silently recited a prayer to the ancestors. Her figure swayed in the fragrant smoke as if she were floating on air. I must confess—I was already drawn to her.

It was the best fish I'd ever eaten. When she placed it before me, I pretended it was too big and I couldn't manage it on my own. I was about to invite the other guests to my table when, to my surprise, I saw that they had all gone. Never mind. I asked Desirée for another beer. Meanwhile, I reached into my rucksack where I kept a handy little box of salt consecrated in our church, carefully sprinkling some on the fish. My final and most important precaution also worked: without hesitation Desirée ate some of the fish with me. This meant she was not intent on casting any spells and, as we chatted, she proved to be a more than pleasant companion. Exactly the kind of woman I like—one who doesn't agree with everything without thinking, but nor does she try to be too clever.

After we parted, I found a decent place to stay, and the next morning went about my work. But she was constantly on my mind and I could barely concentrate on business matters. But to hell with business! I knew I was in love.

We started meeting regularly. Desirée was unlike any other woman I had known. She was unpredictable, an embodiment of all the most wonderful things a woman can be. Every night she wore a different hairstyle, laughed in a different way and was eager to talk about different things. One night she refused to drink any alcohol, the next she had no problem knocking back 10 beers and happily sang along with me on our way home. One evening she wanted to go for roast kanga in a quiet romantic eatery on the shore of the lake, the next she was so insistent on going dancing as if there were no other entertainment in this world. And the raunchy dancing she was into! Another time she seemed pensive and intent on musing, as if the previous days had been wiped from her memory. She was different every time and that's what I found enthralling.

Now I'm again sitting on the shore of the black lake, waiting for her. Will her skin colour today be lightish, or as black as ebony? Will her eyes be brown or black? Will she wear her hair in plaits or down, long and soft as velvet? Will our lovemaking be wonderfully slow, or will we make passionate love like wild animals? Will she smell of fragrant oils, or of smoke like the last time? But she may spring yet another surprise on me. She'll seduce me and once she's wound me around her little finger, she will disappear into the darkness. Or she will appear in the guise of a black kid goat, her eyes aglow . . .

PIMENTOS

Bamenda is some ten kilometres away. It takes me just over two hours to get there. Morning after morning I go to the market there, set up my stall and lay out my pimentoes. Ten bunches, 100 francs each. On a good day, I can make 1,000 francs. There are times when I manage to sell only a bunch or two, sometimes I swap a few of the best for a handful of cassava leaves. When I can see that the pimentoes won't last much longer, I give them to Mariana at the petrol station. You won't find anyone whose pap is as tasty as hers. Men lick all their fingers afterwards and drink more beer than usual.

My daughter's children are sick but she can't afford the medicines. There is no one here I can talk to about it. Everyone has their own problems. Every single woman at the market has something. Every one of us needs money to buy medication or eggs. Rum or beer.

Today I have ten bunches on my tray and I'll be taking ten back. I can't wait much longer, it will get dark soon. I'm too old for this struggle. I start packing up and pretend that I'm crying. But maybe I really am.

At that moment two White men with backpacks come and buy five bunches of my withered pimentoes. At first I'm scared that they might be inspectors but then I see they are holding some banknotes. I bless them. They are my brothers in Christ, I'm sure.

41

HOW DEATH CAME
INTO THE WORLD

Many, many years ago, a man and a woman lived with their children in a hut in a forest. In those days, they were the only people who lived on the earth and the man enjoyed the favour of the gods because he was honest, never harboured any ill intentions, and his children too lived in love and harmony. That is why the gods offered the first man their advice, helped him whenever they could and showed him all kinds of plants that were edible, nutritious and exquisite tasting. They also taught him to hunt so he would always have enough to eat. They initiated him into the mysteries of medicinal plants so that he and his entire family would always enjoy good health and happiness. Should his child ever fall ill, the man would go to the forest and return with a root or some leaves, precisely the ones needed to drive the illness out of the body forever. The gods always told him which part of the plant to use.

The man founded the human tribe and was proud of his descendants who were all hale and hearty and very sensible. Everything would have been fine if, apart from his wife and children, the first man hadn't also had a mother-in-law. At some point she started to give him the evil eye and would try to stir up trouble whenever she came to their yard. She would move things around in the larder and peer into the pots and bags in which the first man kept his magic herbs. The mother-in-law apparently thought that the first man was not good enough to be her daughter's husband and was jealous of his close contact with the gods and forest spirits. But perhaps she had other reasons—after all, who can tell what goes on in a mother-in-law's head? Be that as it may, with each passing year the old woman attempted more and more audacious tricks to make the first man angry and sow discord among his family, so that he would be deprived of the gods' good graces and she would reap benefits for herself.

The mother-in-law's wickedness reached a point where one day she summoned a dormant evil spirit: the rainbow snake. The snake had never had anything to do before—all he did was lounge around in a vast cave on the shores of Lake Wuori waiting for his opportunity to come. The old woman went to find him and told him what bothered her. This was just what the rainbow snake had been waiting for. He came up with a plan to make the first man fall out with his wife. He gave the woman a charm wrapped in a big banana leaf which he told her to unwrap when the first man was nearby and swallow a piece of the magic root without him noticing. What the rainbow snake omitted to mention was that she too would end up paying for all this witchcraft.

The spiteful mother-in-law did as the evil spirit from the cave said: she waited until dusk, when people started to come home from the fields. As the first man approached a pot where she was boiling a hen, she untied the banana leaf and furtively slipped a piece of the root into her mouth. As soon as she felt its peppery taste on her palate, she dropped to the ground, dead as a doornail. When the man's children saw that a root they had never seen before was sticking out of the lifeless woman's mouth, some of them suspected their father of having poisoned her. After all, no one knew herbs better than he did. His wife was more suspicious than most, since she knew that no one but her husband was around when it happened. She made him go into the forest and forage for medicinal herbs that would bring her mother back to life. They had a long argument and when the man failed to convince her that the accusation was false, he headed for the forest and roamed it impotently, imploring the gods to advise him how to bring the old woman back to life. But the gods and the forest spirits remained silent. For not even their magic was able to undo the rainbow snake's witchcraft, as not only had the old woman eaten the poison, but by unwrapping the banana leaf she had let evil out into the world. If it were just a question of bringing someone back to life, there would be plenty of herbs in the forest for doing that. However, from that day on, strife and arguments struck root in the first man's family and death came into the world.

YOLA

He walked along the beach by the ocean. It was a clear and calm moonlit night. He tossed a few stones into the rolling waves and sat down in the sand. And that's when he spotted her. A woman in black emerged from the woods and approached him. He had never set eyes on anything more beautiful.

'I'm Yola and I'm taking you for a swim,' she said.

He didn't mind. In fact, he leapt to his feet as if electrified. He couldn't believe his good fortune. A woman had finally taken notice of him. Just when he stopped begging the water spirits, and his doubting of the gods had become blasphemous. What a stroke of luck! There was justice in this world after all.

'Sure, no problem,' he said and immediately felt embarrassed that he couldn't come up with a more polished reply. How many times had he rehearsed potential conversations in his head and each time it worked like clockwork. He was always ready with a response, studding his answers with ancient pearls of wisdom and embellishing them with smart quips he'd heard from his peers at parties. His sentences flowed as smoothly as love songs. But now all he could muster was 'no problem'.

By the time he collected himself, the woman was already striding into the waves. He quickly stripped off his T-shirt, kicked off his sandals and started to run. As usual, the sea was rough and a few metres from the shore the waves surged almost two metres high. They broke furiously, roaring like an avalanche of rocks in a quarry.

He called out her name, as her figure had vanished into the darkness. No response. He waited for the right moment and plunged over the breaking waves. He found himself out in the open sea and let the waves rock him without having to move his arms as he looked around for Yola.

She surfaced right before him. She gave a mischievous grin and pushed his head under. He breathed out into the water. He wasn't a strong swimmer. He had grown up far from the sea and his parents had never allowed him to swim in the river. That was where evil spirits lived. It was not until he moved here, close to the ocean, that his friends in the factory helped him to overcome his fear of water. He was fairly good at short distances but his technique was still that of a beginner. He liked to splash about in the tide but had yet to master any tricks that were more daring.

As he inhaled the wet force of the ocean, he felt that his head was about to shatter into a thousand pieces. His brain imploded and every muscle in his body went limp. Then he felt the pressure of arms underneath. He lifted his face out of the water. He swore, gave a cough and his eyes started watering. Yola chuckled.

'This must be some sick joke,' he sputtered, trying to pull himself together. He wanted to take a deep breath and explain why he didn't find this kind of joke funny. He saw her bright eyes glinting close to his face and was silenced by a pair of fleshy lips. He was now sailing on quite different waters. As their intertwined bodies drifted in the water, rotating around their axis, he didn't have time even to sigh. At one point he felt that Yola was trying to push him underwater again. He jiggled his legs in terror but she just drew him closer.

The ocean tide impelled them towards the beach and a final, enormous wave washed them ashore. They staggered up onto the sand.

Yola bent down to his freshly scraped knee. She licked the wound and waited for the first tiny drops of blood to ooze out.

He lay next to her, in a state of astonishment. He was in seventh heaven but doubts immediately started to creep in. Who was this Yola? Why was she there with him? What was she after? Could she really be interested in him? Her arms were stronger than anything he had ever come across. He was sure that if she'd wanted to, she could hurl him out of the waves high into the air with just one arm. And those eyes! Now they are kind and smiling, with their pupils shining. But earlier, in the water? What did he see in them in the moonlight?

Slowly, Yola brushed some of the dry sand off his skin. Her quick, skilful movements startled him. He stirred. He felt more awake than ever before. He pulled her towards him. As she straddled him, her outline was all he could make out in the moonlight. His head had emptied of all thought . . . His body was dissolving in the cool sand and his arms embraced Yola along with the trees in his old garden, his sisters and the walls of the house where he was born. He heard plaintive songs from the village church, mingling with the echo of unfamiliar drums that used to put him to sleep when he was young.

'Yo . . . Yola!' he exclaimed in ecstasy. She bent down to him with a long, warm kiss.

'Well then, let's go to my place now,' she whispered into his ear. She stood up, flung her dress over her shoulder and reached a hand out to him.

'It was a dream. It was just a dream,' it flashed through his mind as he stood up mechanically and started to follow the mysterious woman. By now he knew he would never come back to this beach or to the house where he was born. He was going far, far away. With Yola . . .

DEATH AT A PARTY

I came to a small town—the name escapes me for the moment. Dusk was falling, the best time for a glass of Guinness.

In the corner of the bar sat the Grim Reaper, reading a newspaper. The locals tried to ply him with drink of every kind and with other treats, but he refused everything and just sat there with his jaw clenched and poker-faced, like someone waiting to have his revenge. No one in the neighbourhood knew why the Grim Reaper had come to this watering hole but it was immediately obvious to everyone that he must have had a reason.

We were sitting in a small concrete hut, otherwise known as La Cocotte, the local boozer. Huge moths flitting around the kerosene lamp forced you to duck and weave to prevent them from ploughing into your eyes, and it was beneath the lamp that the Grim Reaper sat, biding his time. Whenever someone passed his table for another helping of fufu or to pour themselves some palm wine from a demijohn, they had to give him a wide berth to reach the counter. The Grim Reaper pretended not to care and have no interest in the folks of Douala. He just sat there, one leg (or rather, one leg bone) crossed over the other, puffing on cheap smokes and not joining in the dancing. The bar owner knew that one should be on good terms with death. But as soon as he tried to engage him in small talk, the Grim Reaper would go into a huff and tell him to go to another table.

We spent most of the night drinking. As morning approached, I thought the Grim Reaper was about to leave. He folded his newspaper, which of course made the hubbub die down a bit. No one knew what to expect—anyone could have been the reason why he had been sitting there waiting for his moment. But the Grim Reaper didn't seem to be looking at anyone in particular. As he adjusted his cap, Abe and I thought he would head out into the darkness and we could all relax. But soon we discovered that he hadn't come here just to read his paper and smoke his stinking cigarettes, but that he had a job to do.

One of those dancing, a young woman with plaited hair, suddenly started to gasp and clutch at the great pair of tits that showed through her white T-shirt, emitting what sounded more like a long, low wheeze than a breath, then she kicked her legs up into the air. She just lay on the floor for a while, trembling, but by then the Grim Reaper had begun to lift her onto his back. A really young thing she was.

We didn't know what to do: everyone was taken aback by what we'd witnessed. Until that moment we all thought that the Grim Reaper might change his mind, or that he might have just dropped by for a visit. After all, he would often turn up in the little huts people lived in hereabouts; he would hang around for a while staring at the young children and then leave without further ado. Unannounced, he would observe the terrified families—that was his thing! But lately our folks had got quite used to him turning up. Some would even offer him expensive drinks to get into his good books, and sometimes he did accept a glass and had a little chat with them about this and that, making witty conversation. But this time, at La Cocotte, he really did mean business.

Some of the older women started to scream. They tried to strike a last-minute deal with the Grim Reaper, offering themselves instead. But it was obvious right from the start that this time he wasn't prepared to bargain. There was nothing up for discussion on this night, so we weren't surprised that the old women's pleas went unheard.

The women ran out into the road wailing, hoping to catch up with the Grim Reaper. But no matter how hard they ran, the distance between them kept increasing, even though he seemed to be walking at a leisurely pace. He carried that young slip of a girl clean off. He marched down the path into the darkness, the plaits on the girl's bobbing head giving us one final wave as she dangled from his back.

RIVER

I was delirious for several days. My fever wouldn't abate, the medication wasn't working. I couldn't move and even after sweating it out I couldn't manage more than a few steps around the room in the evening. The doctor's face said it all—he had no idea what was wrong with me and what might help.

Salomon went to the pharmacy and bought something to bring the fever down. I was oblivious of the hours flying by. When I came to, I was in a taxi bumping along in the dark. A late-night calm had already descended on the streets, disturbed only by the occasional honk from a rowdy car driven by a drunk. The car came to a halt in a poor neighbourhood, and Salomon and the driver carried me down a narrow alleyway into a decorated yard. They propped me up against a wall of corrugated metal. Through half-closed eyes filled with tears I registered a bonfire at the centre of a small open space. Its flames danced before me, assuming distorted animal shapes and grinning faces.

They had taken me to the nganga! I forced a desperate smile, but a sudden bout of weakness made me retch. I had heard a lot about the nganga from Bona Beri. How he had healed a feeble-minded boy by pulling a frog out of his head. How he divined the root cause of his patients' problems in his dreams, and then treated them with stones from the river, or cast out their sickness through dance. People told all sorts of stories about him. I used to laugh them off. Some claimed he had found a small box of ritual objects in the woods that someone had buried there for his victim. All he had to do was hack through a small rusty padlock and throw the chain into the water, and a woman who had been infertile conceived within weeks. But now I was prepared to believe anything. I tried to focus on what I was going to tell him, but my head was on fire and my thoughts melted in the flames. I waited, resigned to my fate.

After a short while the nganga emerged from his shack. He wore a long coat and carried a short carved stick. I froze as he came up to me and looked me in the eye. I was incapable of movement because my hands and feet had gone numb. As if I'd been locked inside the stone carapace of my own body. I felt as helpless as a mouse driven into a corner.

I could see nothing but the reflection of the flames in his eyes. They were still and stone cold. The object I had taken for a magic wand unexpectedly came alive. It suddenly twitched in his hand and the tail of a serpent shot out of the tip of his finger. As the nganga stretched an arm out towards me, I saw that it was a real snake. The sorcerer's arm was disappearing down his coat, turning into a body covered in yellow and black stripes. It grew and grew as it came closer. Slowly it wound itself around my chest. Its grip tightened, knocking the wind out of me. Something inside me snapped. I was enveloped in darkness.

I came to in my friend's bedroom. The house was dead silent; only the hooting of cars from a nearby junction could be heard. The sun was already beating down on the windows—I guessed it must have been early afternoon. 'Salomon!' I called out in a feeble voice. I assumed that he and his wife were waiting for me to wake up. The only response was the frightened clucking of chickens in the yard. Nothing suggested any human presence. Could they really have left me here all alone in such a state? I sat up on the edge of the bed. A jug of water and bottles of herbs, a bar of soap and a clean towel had been left on the table. I washed quickly, pulled on my trousers and walked into the yard on unsteady legs. I was feverish, and everything went black in the piercing sun. I stopped and grabbed hold of the fence while I got used to the light. After a while my head stopped throbbing, and I could make out the silhouette of a woman's body at the far end of the yard. Salomon's wife was slaughtering a young goat by the campfire, letting its blood drip into a white plastic bowl. When she was done, she pressed down on an artery with her finger and greedily gulped down the thick blood.

'Hi, Bébé,' I said, approaching. She turned to face me, wiped a bloodstain off her chin with the back of her hand and nodded silently. She went back to her work with an absent expression, leaving me standing there helplessly. I was surprised she showed no sign of being pleased to see that I was better. Whenever we passed each other in the street, she would always flash me a radiant smile, ask how I was, give a laugh and tease me. But just then she didn't even deign to say hello.

'Is something wrong?' I asked uncertainly.

'No. Nothing's wrong. Everything is as it should be,' she replied coolly, ripping out the innards of the goat with one hand.

After a brief pause I said I'd go for a walk until Salomon came back. She didn't even glance at me as I left.

I closed the gate behind me, and after taking a few steps I realized that something must have happened. The street I found myself in looked totally unfamiliar. I didn't recognize anything around me. The warehouse storing mineral water and the barber's on the corner had vanished without trace. In its place stood the painted concrete wall of some business, partly overgrown with moss. I was sure I was outside Salomon's house. I was as familiar with it as with the Mission house where I lived. The patterns on the manholes remained unchanged, as did the view of the top floors of the Parfait Garden hotel, but the bars where we used to hang out had been replaced by deserted shacks and stores selling strange goods. Birds flew in and out of broken windows and hovered above the heads of folk in their Sunday best on their way to the main square. Some kind of festival was about to begin and there wasn't a car in sight. The roads were lined with women dressed in identical purple dresses, the kind worn at funerals. The house fronts were decked out in ribbons and flags of many colours. I asked someone what was going on, but the guy just looked me up and down silently, the way Bébé had done earlier.

I came to a kiosk selling human bones. An old man in a white hat was arranging the bones in rows and chasing away bothersome flies. Bleached skulls gleamed above neatly laid out bones, and heads in various stages of decomposition dangled from the roof. A couple of men stopped by the old man and tried to haggle. I felt feverish again. I ran away.

The crowd grew even more dense at the street corners. A masked procession wound its way along the main street, a band at its head. I stood with my back against a wall and watched the masses of people in their motley shirts. Bodies pressed together as if they were trying to meld and form a single organism. I spotted Salomon standing a few steps away. He managed to give me a cheery wave.

I pushed through the crowd to get closer to him but was caught in a side current that was moving more slowly. I saw Salomon's head disappearing into the distance. I could no longer feel myself walking. I couldn't choose the direction I wanted to go as the crowd swept me uncontrollably out of town, like a twig tossed into a churning river.

I reached the suburb of Bonanjo. I lost sight of Salomon. I tried to fight my way towards him, but I was being pushed relentlessly down the hill by the tide of people. I gave up and went with the flow. Trees flashed past me, and only then did I realize that the road was the same as before, while at the same time being different. An enormous baobab tree loomed where the statue of a football player made of old car parts used to be. The petrol station around the corner was gone, and the taxis honking incessantly had disappeared God knows where. These were places I knew like the back of my hand, yet it felt as if I'd never been there before. A path into a parallel world opened up ahead of me, to another Douala, one that existed independently of my previous life and which I was eager to discover.

The masked people were now at the head of the procession. I was surrounded by many familiar-looking faces, but none of them acknowledged me with a smile, not a single pair of eyes offered a greeting or lingered on me. The only person I felt close to was Salomon, lost among the heads wearing brightly coloured headscarves and old hats.

We crossed Place de la République and turned off towards a ramp leading down to the harbour bridge. Or rather, to what used to be the bridge, as the asphalt road to the Wouri delta was now gone and the riverbank that awaited us was wild and pristine. Instead of a four-lane highway we were descending a muddy path full of potholes and rocks into a valley where the meadow gradually gave way to a mangrove swamp. I didn't ask myself how any of this was possible; it was all too much for one day. My only thought was how to find Salomon. I sometimes stood on tiptoe or jumped up to see if I could spot him anywhere nearby.

In the meadow the crowd dispersed, and I was finally able to come to a stop. To calm down and work out where to go next.

The main current of people was heading for a narrow strip along the riverbank that used to serve as a beach, where Coca-Cola kiosks once stood and the local urchins had kicked a ball around. I'd been there not long ago, watching them. A bunch of older boys had been showing off their tricks and glistening muscles to pretty girls taking cover in the shade of the palm trees. The younger boys imitated their role models. They played with burst rubber balls or fresh coconuts. Barefoot, in shorts, or tattered short pants. I remembered that one of them had no string in his underpants and had to hold on to them with one hand during the game. When the coconut flew into the goal, he joyfully clapped his hands above his head, and his underpants fell to his ankles in front of the whooping girls.

But now the beach wasn't there. Sand hadn't been trucked in and there were no refreshment kiosks. I quickened my pace and pushed my way through the crowd that was no longer so dense, and I could zigzag around people and, above all, keep going in the direction I wanted to go. I was coming close to where the mangroves thinned out, providing the easiest access to the water. I ran ahead a little and watched the people approaching the river. I saw only strange, stony faces, drained of all colour. Only then did I realise that everything around me was grey. It was neither night nor day.

I felt moisture around my sandal-clad feet, which sank into the river mud covered with tiny green flowers. The people around me were wading into the water—slowly, silently, their eyes fixed on the waves. I went along with the crowd, following closely behind a woman in a long white dress. Treading in her footsteps I was able to avoid the sharp rocks at the bottom of the churning river. Waves licked the delicate woollen fabric tightly hugging the curves of the woman's slender legs. I walked at the same pace. I stopped looking back.

I might have walked about 20 yards. I couldn't tell exactly, because the slope was very gentle. I was up to my waist in water when someone grabbed my shoulders from behind. I dragged him along with me for a few steps, convinced that it was someone needing help. Then his grip tightened and his hand gave me an energetic shake. It was Salomon. I was so happy to see him at last: now we could keep walking together. But he pulled me back, anxious to explain something. I couldn't understand a word. His voice was drowned out by the roar of the waves. I tried to lipread and shouted that I couldn't turn back as I was already halfway there, and that he should tell me later.

Despite my protests he eventually managed to drag me out. I scrambled back onto the shore, scraping my legs in several places along the way. Then I collapsed onto the grass, exhausted.

I was woken by piercing sunlight streaming into the bedroom through gaps in the blinds. Taxi drivers' horns were blasting away outside; I could hear laughter and the clamour of street vendors. I was lying under a sweat-soaked blanket, with bags full of roots and compresses soaked in herbal infusions waiting for me on the bedside table. I spotted a pitcher of water and reached for it at once. I was so weak it slipped out of my hands before it touched my lips.

Salomon's eldest daughter dashed in and was soon back with a glass of chilled water straight from the bar. She gave me her usual sad smile and disappeared.

I felt great. I knew I was healed. I pulled on my trousers and went to look for my friends. I was sure Bébé would be out there baking her delicious pastries and Salomon would be in the bar, celebrating my return. I had to join them without delay. Say thank you. I had so much to tell them, and maybe I could even manage the odd sip of beer to celebrate.

I walked through the empty kitchen and opened the door into the yard. A few women from the neighbourhood sat on a bench by the low wall, weeping. So much grief just because someone they barely knew was sick! I was surprised and touched. I was about to make an expansive gesture, open my arms wide and give everyone the great news. Then I saw Bébé. She was shaking in her mother's arms, choking back desperate sobs. Slowly, as I approached, I noticed a few men hanging out in the street, staring at the ground. I began to suspect that the news I would hear might be worse than my own death.

Bébé raised her head and looked at me with red, tearful eyes.

They had found Salomon this morning. He had drowned in the harbour.

FLESH AND BONES

Wa´a ndji a mous mbwembwel wayi wo´o so´
o a nda, a mou na a mous o teou se o djab.

You never know when mbwembwel will pay a visit
to your house. But that day will soon come.

Are you sure you want to hear this? Well then, pour me some of that smooth palm wine first. Then I'll tell you the weirdest thing I've witnessed in my long life. I am 120 years old and you won't find anyone in New Bell who remembers more than I do. Fill my glass to the rim, make sure it has a proper head. Don't leave the can so far away. I have a lot to say and need to find the right words. Without good palm wine I'll just keep rabbiting on. Give us a cigarette. So let's begin.

I was only little when I first heard of graves being plundered. Graves are sacred in these parts, and anyone who desecrates them suffers the worst punishment imaginable. Which is why there was a huge uproar the first time it happened. Someone had dug up freshly buried bodies, leaving them horribly mutilated. I wasn't there but I heard that several people fainted when they saw the ravaged bodies—corpses missing eyes, tongues, hearts and even genitals. Of some of the bodies only headless and limbless torsos remained on the ground.

It was as clear as day that the culprits couldn't have come from our neck of the woods. It was obvious that it was some of those strangers who had moved to our town after the government stumbled upon the mineral deposits. It must have been people who knew the blackest of magic and weren't scared of death. They didn't fear the wrath of the ancestors or the revenge of the gods. And they must have had the help of the most powerful demons, maybe even mbwembwel himself. You see, we weren't dealing just with a bunch of ordinary criminals who would give themselves away and be sooner or later caught by the police. They left no traces and we knew we had to act at once, as our enemy would only grow stronger by the day.

The elders in our old neighbourhood gathered in a hut in the square and stayed up all night discussing what was to be done. The next day the nganga sacrificed a goat and prepared a juju to protect the graves in the Forest of the Dead. A few of the experienced men took turns guarding the graves at night. For the next month or two nothing happened. Everyone was relieved and we thought we could go back to our normal lives. This happened a long time ago, maybe 100 years back, maybe even earlier. I was still very young and I'm not good with numbers. People celebrated in the streets for months, until the start of the rainy season.

But one evening, as I was chasing a ball with the lads from our street, we heard desperate shouting. It was Anuka, the old woman who sold cassava leaves on the corner. She was running through the market place screaming so loud that her voice kept breaking into a funny falsetto. With some difficulty, people managed to stop her but she just kept clapping her hands

61

together, shaking violently as if she was deranged and wailing with her head tilted back: 'Joseph, Joseph!! Oh my God, Joseph!'

Joseph was her son who had died of a heart attack about a month earlier. That day we couldn't prise a sensible word out of her. Long after sunset, she could still be heard in the distance, calling out his name in terror. She obviously couldn't cope with the loneliness after losing her son and had lost her mind. That's what we thought at the time. The doctor gave her some pills to calm her down. Of course . . .

Of course she'd lost her mind, as did many others who would go mad later on. Because, you see, some time later, the dead who'd been buried and mourned a long time ago, suddenly started to appear in the streets. What happened to Anuka was that she saw her late son Joseph walking down the street with an absent look, like a total stranger. His clothes were tattered, but his face was just as she remembered it from the day his stiff body was brought to her on a handcart. She ran towards him, but he didn't react. He was walking mechanically as if he didn't see or hear anything around him.

No one believed her at the time. Not until she persuaded the police to go and check her story out at the cemetery. Joseph's grave was empty. A few months later old Mima, the one who sold baguettes outside the post office, went to see her. She, too, had spent all day weeping, making preparations for a funeral. She tried to avoid the priest so he wouldn't see her visiting the deranged old woman, as that would have been too embarrassing. She left her husband at home, banging his head against the wall and reduced to incoherent rambling. She told Anuka about a dream he'd had that night: he saw his daughter tied up and dragged off into the mountains. In his dream some people came, hauled her out of the bedroom and as she staggered behind them, she knocked over a jug of water. He saw her follow silently in the footsteps of men with shrouded faces. They took her to where the mountaintops reach as high as the storm clouds. She was to work their fields and follow their orders. They had stolen her name, her soul and her body. The dead body they left behind on the mat resembled their daughter only thanks to black magic.

After Mima's husband told her about his dream, they went to their daughter's bedroom and there indeed was the girl's corpse, drenched in water spilt from the overturned jug. They tried to bring her back to life but to no avail. Her husband swore that what he saw in his dream was true and the body lying there was not their real daughter. He pointed to fresh scars on her stiff body, neck and arms and an unnaturally arched belly that seemed to have been emptied completely long ago. He insisted that this was not their daughter but a fake fashioned out of other people's bodies . . .

Old Anuka listened and nodded in agreement. The flame of truth blazed in her eyes. The mutilated bodies in the graves, her disappeared son and Mima's daughter—all this was connected.

Would you have believed this kind of story? We all thought it was just crazy talk. But it doesn't matter whether you believe something or not. The world doesn't give a damn what you think.

More and more reports of similar cases emerged. No one believed them at first but we had to live with them. We offered up sacrifices to our ancestors so that they would punish the culprits and restore order to our lives. Because this was the kind of thing everyone was more terrified of than of death. But our ancestors were clearly not powerful enough to put an end to this chaos. Suddenly our jujus no longer worked and our dead relatives stopped answering our prayers. Rivers of white cockerels' blood were spilt, the soil by the Sacred Forest soaked up litres of spirit and our shrine was filled with sacrifices. But news of grave robberies kept coming and all the people at the market talked about was another dead person that someone had recently spotted in the street and mysterious folk prowling about at night with huge bundles on their backs. Rumour had it that the bundles were filled with the human limbs and phalluses they needed for their black magic. It gave them their power as well as the ability to bring the dead back to life and force them to become their slaves. People started locking their doors at night and windows were left shuttered till dawn even on the hottest and muggiest days. No one wanted to risk falling into the clutches of the mbwembwel himself. My mother forbade me to play anywhere other than our street and I ended up spending my days in the courtyard with two kids from our compound, seeing my friends only at school. I was fed up but didn't dare disobey. I saw too much fear in the faces of adults absorbed in heated discussions.

Time dragged on until one day old Anuka showed up with her latest news. Since she hardly slept at night, she sat by the window and through a crack in the shutters she espied an old woman and two men hurrying towards the road leading to Edea, carrying bundles on their backs. 'They must be from Edea! I knew it! And I bet it was the body parts of our folk, stolen from the cemetery in the Sacred Forest, that they carried in those bundles. They use them to assemble living corpses who then carry out their orders!' she shouted to the group of people gathered around her.

Some just shook their heads in disbelief and said it could have been just vagrants of some kind. But most believed Anuka's explanation. It all fitted together. It explained why the Edeans were so well off. You could instantly tell them from everyone else at the market, so cheerful, rested and prinked out they were. They obviously spent all day lounging about while their soulless slaves did all the hard work for them.

People stood in their doorways talking until night fell. The bravest men organized a vigil by a window after agreeing secret signals to summon everyone to a previously agreed place at the appropriate moment. We couldn't wait any longer since it felt as if mbwembwel was tightening a noose around our town that was certain to kill us all. It was only a matter of time before he paid a visit to your own or your neighbour's house.

Finally, the night arrived. The men who kept watch spotted a pair of strangers prowling close by the walls to avoid the moonlight. They wore long coats and had bundles on their backs. The watchmen gave the signal and sprinted after the two men. A few streets down they caught the strangers. And they didn't mess about, believe you me. One was stabbed and another died of fear, I think. But there was nothing in the bundles but goods from the grocery warehouse. Tins, maize flour and some rum in a few plastic bottles. People slowly gathered around and stared in silence at the dead bodies of the two miserable wretches. That night, I had very disturbing dreams and I woke up to the sound of laughter. A nasty belly laugh that gave me the chills.

And then it was over. However, nothing in our town has ever been the same since. People rarely laugh much these days. Many have stopped offering up sacrifices. And hardly anyone believes anyone else. Just like you don't believe my story.

A DESPERATELY
WONDERFUL LIFE

David woke up feeling that something was not right. Last night he had lain down on his mattress as a strong man in his prime, and now he had awoken as a woman. He had a pair of breasts like he'd always desired and admired in women in his neighbourhood. His hips were a bit too wide for his taste though. They were as voluptuously rounded as the hips flaunted by the Bantele sisters who ran the mango stall on the corner. A little harmless banter, followed by a slap on the bottom, then off he'd go with a chuckle—this was his regular bit of fun on his way to work.

He sauntered up and down in front of the mirror. He felt like a duck, waddling clumsily from side to side.

'What's this supposed to mean? What's this supposed to mean?' he kept mumbling under his breath. He wondered how the guys in the bar would react to his transformation. They'd guffaw. They'd slap him on the bottom while he stood at the bar dressed in a floral skirt. Will it be fun? Is a woman supposed to drink so much?

He was anxious as he walked into the bar. It was quite early and none of the regulars had arrived yet. He ordered a beer and savoured it in long, thirsty swigs. He smacked his lips contentedly.

Soon his neighbour turned up with Philip, who'd got promoted today. A bottle of rum appeared on the counter, and there was a free round for everyone. His neighbour didn't recognize David. He just slammed his glass down on the table with a laugh and a suggestive wink. David was about to return the smile but then checked himself. He downed his drink in one go.

'Starting an affair with a neighbour is the last thing I need,' he thought. 'He goes out with a woman every night. And a different one every time!'

David will need to give this some thought. Actually, dammit. No need to think. He's not going to give his body to just anyone. He's not going to give it to anyone at all!

He paid up quickly and hurried out into the street. He knew that if he had another drink, he would give himself away, making this wretched situation even more complicated.

He gazed at himself more and more frequently, taking longer and longer. He would approach the mirror aglow with anticipation. He tried on various clothes and wrapped himself in fabrics of many colours. He chose and compared patterns carefully. Only now did he realize that he'd become aware of himself as a physical being. Before he'd never noticed his belly sticking out over his belt. He couldn't remember what kind of T-shirts he used to wear as a man. Now he paid attention to every fold of his skin. He found the sight more and more appealing. And then it dawned on him. He was in love.

Within a few days he adopted the manners of a lady from a good family and began to burn through the savings he kept carefully hidden in a crack in the plyboard behind the mattress. His own voice could be heard less and less. He felt he was now under the complete control of this other, stronger self. He had become a stranger in a new body, into which his own conscious-ness slowly disappeared. He no longer had the strength to speak out and resist. He watched his new mistress in horror. He was now merely the source of energy that lent this woman her strength.

He watched her shop for herbs in the market. He looked on as she carefully placed dried chameleons into her basket and wrapped bones in newspaper. Cast flirtatious glances at young men. She usually picked a lonesome man in the crowd and with-out herself making a move waited for him to notice her. Their eyes would meet and David always felt a chilling excitement he was ashamed of. He knew she was choosing a new victim. All he managed was some feeble curses drowned out by the chaos. Each encounter of this kind left him weaker. He was getting lost in fear.

The night before his strange transformation he had bumped into a striking woman in the market. She carried a wicker basket on her shoulders and looked him up and down provocatively. He was more attracted to her than to any other woman he'd ever met—even though she made him feel quite anxious. When their eyes met, he gave a shudder.

That night she appeared to him in a dream. As she entered his room, he recoiled and shivers ran down his spine. He was unable to move or utter a word. He just lay in bed, gazing into her eyes. He felt a mix of excitement and fear. He was naked and felt awkward.

He wanted to kick her out. To shut his eyes. Tell her off. But instead he just dissolved in the enormous pupils of her eyes.

As she came closer, a wave of heat washed over him. Smiling, she took off her dress and bent down towards him.

Come Saturday morning she was out on the hunt again. She didn't so much as glance at David's limp body, starting to rot in the back room.

THE FAREWELL DANCE

A garage in the centre of Douala. Two gangsters are torturing a man.

'I don't know what you're talking about.'

'Big mistake, man. That's not how we do things around here. We're quick off the mark here.'

'But I really have no idea . . . '

'No idea? Tough luck.'

A brutal uppercut on the chin, followed by a thorough thrashing. Once the man is beaten to a pulp, one of the gangsters raises his head and says:

'See, you could've spared yourself all this if you'd remembered straight away.'

The man doesn't answer. He's covered in blood.

'Is he alive?'

'Don't know, but no one has lasted this long.'

'What if he really had no idea?'

'Well, that really would be tough luck. It would mean he got done for no reason. If I were in his shoes, I'd prefer to be the cool guy who's taken his secret to his grave.'

'We'll have to ditch him somewhere.'

The gangsters pick the man up and carry him out into the street. One of them hails a taxi. A cabbie pulls over, rolls down his window and asks:

'What's wrong with this guy? Cause I don't take corpses.'

'Ha, a corpse! Can't you hear him? He's snoring away. His wife will dress his wounds and he'll be fine.'

'Where to?'

'Same difference. Just drive, see where we get.'

The cab takes off and drives through one neighbourhood after another. The streets are teeming with people, there are no empty alleyways to reverse into and get rid of the cargo. They can't leave him in the middle of the road. After more than half an hour they finally find a suitable pile of rubbish at the far end of the market. They pull him out by the legs and cover him with cabbage leaves.

'He'll sleep it off and everything will be OK.'

Despite their reassurances, it has now dawned on the cabbie that there's no way this fellow's wife will dress his wounds ever again. The men paid their fare simply by letting him live. The 1,000 francs on top will be just enough for him to park his old Toyota somewhere and get a few decent drinks.

I wake up coughing. My face is buried in a pile of rotten oranges, my body is crawling with ants and worms. I stick my head out of a blanket of cabbage leaves and feel my battered body with my hands. I have to have a wash and treat my wounds. Then I'll find the bastards who did this as well as the man who sent them.

My mother doesn't recognize me. She gets up from the table in shock and stares at me open-mouthed. I look in the mirror. I can't blame her. I'm covered in blood and my face is swollen. I splash some water over myself in the yard and put on clean clothes. I disinfect the wounds with some cologne and go to see the people of the ibogа. It's Saturday, I have to hurry if I am to get hold of the shaman before preparations for the ritual begin. The ngozé starts at high noon. I pass through a gate at the end of our street. I press a bundle of banknotes into the shaman's hand and tell him what it is I want to find out. He can ask on my behalf but I will need to be present.

A garden soon after sunset. I'm among a crowd strolling around the iboga shrubs. Kaolin-painted faces are lit up by torches. Their light is absorbed by women's eyes that start to shine in the darkness like the eyes of big wild cats. Bowed figures writhe in agony, their eyes rolled back with their whites showing. The shaman wraps a rock in a banana leaf, ties up the bundle with a strip of bast and sets it down in the middle of the straw hut. I'm dressed in a white bubu like everyone else here. I repeat words that mean nothing to me. I don't know this language, this is the first time I've attended this ritual. I've come to ask the ancestors for the answer to a single question. I watch the throng of women dancing in ecstasy as the musicians get their instruments ready. The shaman crawls into a tent. I help carry food from the kitchen to a festively laid table. A feast for the dead and the spirits.

I wait. I see a host of white figures slowly emerge from the dark bushes. The drumming prevents me from thinking. A man next to me shudders spasmodically, all the veins on his body are swollen, his muscles bulging.

Then the shaman steps out of the tent and unties the strip of bast on the banana leaf. Instead of the rock it contains a little pool of clear water. He drinks it. Now he is ready to share with us what he has gleaned from talking to the dead. In the early hours I discover the name of the man who had sent these guys after me. He is Bo Orowu, a merchant. I'd never heard that name before.

A residence surrounded by a high wall topped with barbed wire. I walk past a guard with a gun slung across his shoulder. He doesn't see me. I run across the garden with a pool and bushes trimmed in the French style. I finally find him on the first floor in a study crammed with heavy mahogany furniture.

'I hope I'm not disturbing you,' I say once I'm standing right in front of his desk.

He raises his head from his papers. His eyes widen and he starts coughing. He lets his cigarette drop on the carpet.

'You are . . . you are . . . ' he stutters, as if choking.

'Yes, I'm the one you had killed. I've come to find out why you did it,' I say slowly and watch his hands as he rummages, terrified, in a drawer in his desk. I know that no gun can help him.

But he is too weak to put up any resistance. His heart seems to have failed. He tries to catch his breath a few times, in loud bursts. Then he freezes and his head droops, eyes bulging.

His trembling hand clutches a juju. There's nothing more for me to do here.

Almost two days have passed, I don't have much time left. One end of the sky is turning a purplish red. A grey-blue cloud approaches from the other, bringing darkness. Esterla used to say that a red sky conceals tears and blood, which are about to be covered with the grey of forgetting and indifference. That is how one forgets suffering. By throwing pain and sadness away at night.

My last dance. I am hugging the only woman in my life, every woman in this world. She holds me close with her body from every side, her arms form a strong, warm rope around me, tying it into a knot across my shoulder blades. Her hard nipples press into my chest and all I have to do is let myself be carried by the pace she dictates. I feel her legs on my knees but also on my back. She is all around me.

Her eyes shine by the light of the paraffin lamps and the traces her feet leave in the sand are no bigger than those of a lion cub. If I still had a heart, this is where I would leave it.

It's late. Time for me to go.

I'LL JUST SIT AND WATCH

I'll just sit down on this rock and stay here all night long, looking. From where I'm sitting I can see a few mud huts, some orange groves to one side, a forest with papaya trees jutting out on the other, and between them a path leading to the lake.

Once I have sat down, it won't be easy to get me out of here. And why would anyone want to do that anyway? No one will pay me the slightest attention. I will just sit and watch. Wait and listen. To the pitter-patter of ants, the screaming of hyenas, the shrieking of monkeys, the snoring of old men, the humming of the wind.

It's been a long time since I was last here. It's hard to believe how quickly people forget. Just the other day, not quite 50 rainy seasons ago, I lived here, in a hut with my three sons. One after the other they left and our house became water logged. The wall by the kitchen disappeared, the roof caved in. To say nothing of the shed and the granary: they collapsed in a heap, and the wind scattered the topsoil every which way. And now my neighbours—the bastards—have built their outhouses where my hut once stood!

But that's not what I was going to say. I know many who return to this world regularly, for a chat with their kin. Years ago, on Saturdays, I too would sometimes summon my father back so he could look around and offer his advice. We would have a drink together. Now he is far away and has other duties to attend to.

My sons live in town, a strange, distant place. If I could turn the clock back to when they were young, I would give them a thrashing in advance. I'd teach them a lesson. Now they dress in the crisply ironed shirts of White people and drive around on wheels, shouting and rushing from one place to another all day long. They never have a thought to spare for their father. And why should they summon me back if they can't even talk to their own wives and children? Do you think they will return one day? I used to come here and wait for them on this rock, but I've given up all hope. But one day we will have words.

It is dark and I have the world before me all to myself. The trees' canopies have bowed down, casting shadows that resemble the most outlandish creatures in the moonlight. This is one reason why people lie low in their huts. They are startled every time they hear some rustle from the forest and imagine spirits gathering around the village. It's been a very long time indeed since I last saw an evil spirit around here. Yet the people are as frightened as little children and still do nothing to remain on good terms with the spirits. They are scared of being punished. It's never occurred to them that what they ought to be scared of are the living—themselves.

Tonight is a really beautiful night.

I don't need anything. All I need is to sit and watch.

And to haunt.

And if I spot a person going to the outhouse before dawn, perhaps I'll take him along with me, to the other side.

THE BLAZE

I've never talked about this. To anyone. Every time I passed its walls, I would be gripped by a strange feeling. Fear. No, that's not the right word. Awe, rather, of a kind I have never felt anywhere else. Let me give you an example: I didn't dare spit when I went past, not until I got to the end of the road and turned towards the market, where it was out of sight for a while. Although I was just a six-year-old given to spitting all over the place while learning to smoke cigarettes: one step, one spit. I used to spit like an old drunk. If you'd followed in my footsteps on the way to school, you could tell by the spittle in the dust whether I had made it to the classroom or bunked off. I wanted to be like my father who hung around bars nursing his beer and lobbing gobs of spit big enough to knock a rat over. My own gobs weren't as dense and compact, saliva just came gushing out of my mouth like water from a well. Every time I lit a cigarette, it would collect under my tongue in such quantities that I had to spit it out or swallow it; it almost made me sick.

But that's not what I wanted to say, I was going to tell you about the church. The only reason I mentioned the spitting was to explain the strange effect this building had on me. I'd be on my way to school, inhaling the dark brown smoke from a roll-up and suddenly, as I passed the stone wall of the church, something inside me would buck. Like a mule rearing up in the middle of the road regardless of how hard its master is thrashing it. I felt an irresistible urge to spit, my mouth was brimful of acrid saliva, but something held me back. I just couldn't bring myself to spit near the church. I was scared that I might desecrate the hallowed soil, although I don't have a rational explanation for this, since all I knew about God back then was what our new teacher managed to tell us. And I couldn't make head or tail of that. God created the earth, plants, animals, human beings and, finally, Jesus Christ. A White man who sacrificed his life for us Black people, too. Most of the little we were taught in religious education and were supposed to learn by heart just didn't add up. It defied logic. Take the countless number of angels who live in heaven: they are as white as fresh fufu, with not a single angel from my country in sight. The devils, on the other hand, are all as black as night, like me. And God is angry with them. It didn't make any sense. Why are there only White people in heaven and why is evil as black as my face?

On our street there are quite a few drunks who beat their wives, yet there are also people like Maria. The one who runs the bar opposite our house. She has never harmed a soul and has done many good deeds to boot. She shares leftovers with people who have come to our town from the countryside in search of work—there is no work in our town. Why should anyone be angry with her and want to punish her? As far as I'm concerned, Maria has definitely earned a place in heaven. If there's justice in the world, she ought certainly to turn into an angel.

I tried to picture her as an angel. A black angel floating above the streets, her orange dress with its animal-mask pattern billowing in the early evening breeze. Every now and then she would swoop down on a bar brandishing her dirty rag and inadvertently sweep fishbones off the table. Why should she end up in hell like all the black devils in the illustrated Bible?

And what about me? Should I end up there just because I sometimes spit near the church? I couldn't understand what held me back and had no explanation for my awe of the walls of Don Bosco. As if it had been deeply ingrained in me before I was even born. Just one look at its red bricks and bang! Was that an inkling of things to come?

Then that day arrived. I was walking home from school, looking forward to going to see a film with my friend Ben in the evening. We'd been collecting empties all over town for a whole week and had finally scraped together enough money to buy two tickets in the back row. The best spot, where no one can see you, but you see everything from your ringside seat. You can watch the couples in love, throw orange peel at the girls or watch the movie. I saw myself proudly walking past the usher who would give a respectful bow and show me to my seat. Then I would sit there, my feet on the seat in front.

Suddenly the church bells started to ring out loudly. Everyone looked in their direction, startled, as the bells weren't ringing the full hour and neither was it time for mass. The old, cracked bell rang out so loud it made my temples throb.

A blaze of light appeared above the church. Fierce and scorching. As if the sun were suspended directly above the church spire. Rays brighter than anything I'd ever seen before illuminated the outlines of houses in the street, bouncing off the corrugated iron roofs. The dark silhouette of the church glowered at us from the hill above. Threatening, unforgiving.

One after another people screwed up their eyes and crossed themselves. An older man in front of me clutched at his heart and dropped to the ground. There was no time to attend to him, to offer help. A commotion broke out with people running every which way. I also took to my heels. I bounded down the hill and turned into the nearest winding alley. I hid behind the latrines and watched the blood-red sky. Mothers trembled as they peered out fearfully from behind window blinds, beggars pressed pieces of cardboard to their chest as if someone was about to rob them, dogs yowled and chickens dashed headlong left, right and centre.

I thought the streets would ignite from all the heat.

I don't know how long I stood there, turned to stone, before I suddenly realized I was staring at a girl crouching behind a window across the street. The blinds on the kitchen window, left slightly open, drew lines across her face. And what I saw in her eyes was different from the horror I'd seen in those of the people running down the streets. It was sheer helplessness and sadness.

I wanted to wave to her but thought better of it. At that moment I realized that my teacher was right. We are here to suffer and hell awaits us.

PUSHING THE LIMITS

'No, thanks. Just the one beer, I've had my fill,' says Raphael as his sits down at his regular table whose wonky legs have needed propping up for the past 10 years. 'Or I'll be sick.'

He comes every day, for this is the most beautiful place in the world. It has a fridge and a view of the valley. A seat by the stream, with all of life laid out before him.

Yesterday he was here at his neighbour's wake. Women wept, men drank rum and reminisced. None more so than Rafael. He and Woli had been the best of friends.

For hours they sat at the rickety table. Rafael kept kissing his friend's grey hair and cold hands. He had a drink with everyone. He corrected the eulogists and added details to the stories they told. He wanted to remember but also to forget. He shouted into the darkness about how extraordinary Woli's ordinary life had been. He sang and danced, tilting his head so far back that he could wave to the stars. He longed to commit the stories he heard to memory while at that same time wanting to empty his head of all such memories. Forget the nights at the Solution Bar. But there isn't enough rum in this world.

He had more than enough. And today he's the worse for wear.

He takes a sip from the chilled bottle and gives a sigh. The kind of sigh old men left alone in this world relieve themselves of. Woli's eldest daughter turns up on the terrace. The one whose calves he was secretly crazy about. The thought now made him blush.

'I liked the way you talked about my father last night. Let's have a drink,' she says and places a shot of strong home-distilled brandy in front of him. Rafael knows he ought to step on the brakes. If he drinks this, things are not going to end well. But, as if on autopilot, he does as the woman asks—he lifts the glass to his lips and the pungent smell of alcohol knocks him hard. He throws up everything he ate last night. The table is covered in the stuff.

'Now that's what I call a proper gent. A customer who knows exactly when he's had enough,' says the bartender and fishes a rag out of a bucket. The place needed a clean anyway.

HOW TO DANCE
THE MAKOSSA

Kolmar is walking down the street slowly, dragging his feet. He's just had a big bowl of pig's innards with a huge portion of spicy groundnut pap and his belly is bloated. Nothing can make Kolmar walk fast when his belly is full. Even if, out of the corner of his eye, he were to spot a leopard on a tree in front of the church lying in wait for its prey, he would just shrug his shoulders dejectedly and continue at the same pace, accepting his fate. So what if he was eaten. That's just the way of the world.

It's the same way now. He lifts one foot and it takes him ages to take even the slightest step forward. He pauses by the street sellers carrying bowls on their heads laden with treats, biscuits, batteries and combs. The sight of roasting fish makes his mouth water. It looks so fresh and tempting. He swallows, as if testing his stomach. There isn't much room left but he might just manage to force down a tiny mackerel . . . He picks a piece that will fit into the palm of his hand and keeps an eye on the street seller to make sure she roasts the fish properly and doesn't skimp on the palm oil. He puts it on a piece of greaseproof paper, sprinkles some chopped onion over it and takes his time examining it from every side. Then he munches it down, still boiling hot, in a bite or two and tops it off with a sprig of matured cassava. He washes everything down with a glass of water and continues on his way.

Today is a holiday and Kolmar is going to the stadium. There will be dancing, bands, acrobats and magicians performing tricks with scorpions and footballs. It's still only midday, he has plenty of time to saunter around.

He stops to wipe the beads of sweat from his brow with a paper tissue and watches the street's hustle and bustle. A boy is riding down the hill in a two-wheel cart, terror in his eyes, an ecstatic, racing-driver smile on his lips. He's hurtling along so fast that his ears are flapping in the wind and his backside slams into the wooden planks on the bumpy road. Just before he reaches the main road, he gives the steering shaft a skilful twist and the cart rotates around its axis a few times at breakneck speed. As it brakes, the cart kicks up dust and an angry mango seller bashes the young driver on the head with an empty cardboard box. Kolmar smiles and applauds the boy. Not many people would dare ride down a slope that steep! When he was young, he also had a go at it but he could never keep his balance on two wheels attached to the middle of the sides of the cart.

'Bravo!' he shouts and gives the boy a cheerful wave.

He continues towards the stadium down a road lined with palm trees. One can stop and relax in their shade and have a moment's rest from the sun. He shouts at some girls who have overtaken him, their long floral dresses billowing in the pleasant breeze as if in greeting. He chats up a couple of women students. He gives them directions to the gig and tells them when Kotto Bass, their favourite act, will be on. But they soon leave him behind, as his pace is too slow for their long, impatient legs. Never mind, there's no rush. He'll bump into them again and then he'll show them how to dance the makossa! Young people can no longer dance the way he did in the old days. You have to let yourself be carried by the rhythm, feel it with the whole of your body, but move only your hips, that's the way to do it. You have to dance slowly, making your every move speak. These days everyone just shakes themselves about, the young dollies showing off their bums and the guys grinding against them. That has nothing to do with the real makossa! Just wait till the evening!

He saunters slowly between stalls with fruit and alcohol. He savours the smells that are more intense in the early morning air than at any other time of the day. At the end of the street, right by the entrance to the stadium, he sees a small huddle around a man in a white lab coat not letting their eyes off him. The man, bedecked with shiny beads, is demonstrating the miracles of medicine. He's passing around samples for a free trial.

'Forty-seven herbs mixed into a unique medication that's unlike anything in the history of mankind! Only a thousand francs, this single little box will get rid of hundreds of ailments. Of the stomach, skin, women's illnesses, sexually transmitted diseases, you name it. What? Yes, it works for AIDS as well, of course! You'll feel better in less than ten days!'

The man pitches his goods confidently and with a smile. He is sure of his success. He holds his arms above his head. In one hand he has the box with the magic red medication, with the other he waves a piece of paper about. 'This certificate is proof that my medicine is genuine. It was issued by doctors in America. Headache? No problem. All you need to do is dab a tiny bit on your temples, like so, and I guarantee you'll feel better in minutes. Women's issues? A thin layer will do the trick. Your teeth? Put a little bit on the tip of your finger and massage your gums.

Dysentery or constipation? Swallow a spoonful and your problem will vanish. TB, AIDS? Same thing, just take a few more spoonfuls, between two and ten, depending on the stage of the disease. My medicine is so clever it can tell what's ailing you and will take care of it. Well then, anyone like to try? A sample is free and today is a holiday, a box will set you back just 1,000 francs! You may think I'm crazy to be selling something so precious so cheap. But 1,000 francs is a special price just for today! Only 1,000 francs and you'll be as good as new, happy and healthy, with nothing ailing you. Any takers?' A forest of arms reaches for the sample box. The doctor comes closer and asks people what ails them. He applies a little on someone's brow, smears more on someone else's belly, and others dip their finger into his miracle cure and have a taste. Beaming with joy, people are taking their wallets from their pockets and from under their skirts. The boxes are disappearing fast, some people buying as many as 10. Kolmar pushes his way forwards anxiously, a scrunched up 1,000-franc note in his hand. He is seriously concerned that he might end up empty handed. It would be a good idea to always have this kind of medicine handy, just in case. At last it's his turn and he dips his finger in and has a lick of the blood-red jelly. It tastes quite nice, like liquorice. He elbows his way out of the crowd. Once he's out of the melee, he dips his fingers into the jelly-like stuff a few more times, licks his fingers clean and stows the magic medicine away in his pocket. He has no health problems but it might do something for his bloated stomach! Good digestion is the foundation of every great feast.

He takes a few steps and feels a burning sensation in his stomach. He breaks out in a sweat. A wave of heat sweeps rapidly through his whole body. Maybe it's the miracle cure already at work? It feels as if a mixture of chilli and detergent were bubbling inside him. He wipes his brow with his last tissue, arms and legs trembling.

He feels like shouting, yelling, flying. Somewhere deep down a voice in his subconscious wonders what's happening to him. What's happening to his muscles, his willpower? What's got into him and where is he rushing? Every cell in his body is infused with a kind of energy he has never known. He feels that any minute now he'll burst and fly off into the crowd.

At the stadium entrance he spots the group of students he met earlier. He starts running towards them, his gait unnatural and comical. He has not run since he was a young boy and now his arms are flailing about clumsily. As he leans forward zigzagging through the crowd, his knees give way now and then, twisting painfully out of their sockets. His bulging eyes gleam in the darkness.

Sounds of music come pouring from every direction and female figures caper about in the lamplight. He can't wait, he has to dive into a bar as soon as possible. He wants to see himself bounce up and down on the counter with the slimmest and most beautiful girl. He knows he won't find a decent place to dance. But it doesn't matter now. It makes no difference. Any dirty old hut will do. He'll dance with a girl from Ebolowa! You won't understand unless you've met a girl from Ebolowa, a child from Ebolowa, a mother from Ebolowa. He has to find one as soon as possible, plant his arms around her waist and pull her towards him.

He hears the makossa. His heart is pounding to its rhythm. He feels the urge to hug everyone, to share the enjoyment of the rhythm, hear them laugh and shout up to the sky. Mosquitoes are pricking him as never before but he's oblivious of everything except female curves. His gaze is glued to their swaying skirts, the cheap market-bought fabric with forest and animal prints.

He storms into a bar and leaps onto a table.

'Makossa!' he yells to the whirl of the drums, wildly swaying his pelvis. In a trance, his head tilted far back and grinning like a lunatic, he pulls the belt from his trousers and swings it round high above his head. People laugh at his lascivious gestures. Everyone's eyes are glued to him.

Before long the owner storms in. Seeing him with his trousers down and around his ankles, he shakes the table and yells: 'This is a decent bar! Go fuck yourself somewhere in the bushes, or I'll kill you!'

Kolmar doesn't hear any of the swearing. He's not taking in anything but the sounds of percussion and the women sprawling about in his fantasies. 'Makossa!' he yells, getting entangled in his trousers and tumbling to the ground. The bar owner gives him a few slaps with a wet rag, earning enthusiastic applause. He staggers out into the fresh air.

Outside he quickly does up his trouser buttons and spots a small group of women by the stalls. 'Uaaaau!' he yells, charging towards them, head down. People step out of his way in surprise, some women laugh in their partner's embrace, others run away with a shriek. Kolmar feels he's going to burn to a cinder if he doesn't catch a girl immediately. He wants to demonstrate the dance at which no one is as good as he is. Why are they all running away? 'Stop!'

Everyone stares at him, the perv, the madman.

A DAY DRENCHED IN WATER

One evening Douala was struck by a horrendous storm. The high winds shattered several banana trees by the bridge, before battering the wooden huts in Bona Beri. People deprived of their roofs by the wind screamed for their lives, but nobody could hear them. The tempest roared like an airplane engine, and rubbish swirled through the air high above the streetlamps. Then came a flash of lightning and water came down in torrents from the sky.

The rain pounded the roofs so hard that even in Maria's bar it was impossible to talk. People cowered silently under the concrete roof and stared at the puddles under the cars and the huge pothole in front of the Hotel Pinel across the street. Everyone here was used to thunderstorms and water ripping the odd piece of tarmac out of the road, but this time it looked as if not just the asphalt road but even the drains in front of their houses would be washed away. Even though the rainy season wasn't due for quite a while.

Green figures could be seen flitting beneath the streetlights. They were the spirits of those who had left the world burnt up by fever. Every time malaria or yellow fever drove someone to their death, their spirit would fly off so that it didn't burn in the heat. It would reappear only when it rained, for the water to cool it down a bit. But on that day, it rained so hard that even spirits such as these would grumble and curse.

Maria was grumpy since she hadn't managed to clear the chairs from the pavement in time. Two were blown away and smashed on a neighbour's wall. Gripping a barely smouldering cheap cigarette between her wet fingers, she watched in silence as the water surged into her bar—a mouldering garage with holes for windows. By now we were ankle deep in water but Maria didn't even stir to rescue the bags of yams and cassava in the kitchen. Frightened rats emerged from every corner and scurried frenziedly around our feet. Just then a curious trader appeared by the entrance. He carried on his head a basin filled with nuts, condoms, soaking batteries and sachets of cheap booze dangling from its sides. No one had any idea how he'd managed to make it as far as the bar in this weather. Although the gale had let up slightly, it was still powerful enough to make the electric lampposts in the street lean over, and if a child or a slim adult had ventured out, they would have been blown all the way to the ocean. Yet, the trader was a diminutive old man no one had ever seen here before. The bowl sat on his head as if glued to it and it didn't even wobble in the wind.

So the nut seller came in and put his bowl down on a table. A few peanuts were floating in the murky water. He gestured for us to help ourselves. He said he'd picked them from his own garden. His head, covered with a small piece of folded cloth supporting the bowl, also resembled a damp peanut roasting under the faint flickering lightbulb around which mosquitoes and moths were careening. We all felt strangely attracted to this man. Several of us dipped our hands in and scooped up some peanuts. They were fresh and raw, their skin caked with a thick layer of mud.

The downpour eased a little and it was now possible to make out other sounds in the bar. The fellow made himself comfortable in a chair and announced that we had to pay for the peanuts. Some of us exchanged baffled glances, for it went without saying that a trader would charge for his wares. 200 CFA for a cup of peanuts. But he launched into an explanation in a tired guttural voice, saying that he wanted much more and that we could stick our 200 CFA where the sun doesn't shine. He said he preferred to be paid in the form of the girl in a greenish-yellow skirt who had rushed into the bar seeking shelter from the storm. She hadn't drunk anything until now and just stood by the counter waiting. But the girl wasn't happy about this kind of barter and started shrieking and swearing.

The two of them got into an argument. Eventually, Maria decided to step in. She grabbed a broom and waved it at the drenched man, splashing us with mud and tiny worms. The man backed into a corner and stood there gawping for a while, then bounded out into the rain making threatening gestures with his bowl as he moved away. Then lightning struck, and he climbed up it into the sky. This was the storm's final bolt of lightning. Once it was gone, the wind and the rain died away as well.

THE SHADOW

Gingerly, Philip pokes his head round the door. He is in luck. It's cloudy outside, the street is ready for rain. He can venture out among people.

Music is blasting out of speakers in front of the bars. People sit and drink, chilling out after work. They scoop pieces of pork skin out of pots and roast them over charcoal having coated them with a thick layer of spices. They gulp down their food almost without chewing. The spices are infernally hot. They sweat profusely, sharing smiles with their neighbours. Night is falling.

Philip orders a bottle of Coca-Cola and buys a few sachets of rum at a kiosk. He downs one, pours the rest into the Coca-Cola bottle and stirs it. Now he can relax. He can lean back in his chair and stretch his legs. The tension has eased, the sun is setting slowly. There's a man sitting opposite him, he can have a chat. The shadow won't show up again today.

It all began a few days ago. Philip was at the till, feeling bored as he looked out at the sleepy street. His shop was empty, like it had been for most of this month. About 10 women had come to stock up with a few tins but otherwise business was poor. A young thief ran past, chased by several shopkeepers. The din startled Philip out of his torpor. He rubbed his eyes and glanced at the big clock above the door. It was just after three. Still ages until closing time.

Slowly he began to sink into a state of stupor. Mechanically, he counted the bricks on the wall under the ancient, peeling plaster. Just then the shadow appeared on the wall for the first time. It lingered there for a while before heading towards the boulevard. Philip waited for the figure casting the shadow to emerge, but no one passed his shop. He looked out but the road was empty. So he had a shot of liquor and convinced himself that it was just his imagination. He shut up shop earlier than usual.

The second time he saw the shadow was at the market. This time it was much more substantial and what baffled Philip was that he was the only one to notice it. Crowds of people were milling about. A new delivery of zuu, the cheap crude oil, had just arrived. You couldn't get anywhere near the lorry. Traders bashed each other on the head with cans and hoses flew in the air like confetti at a party. Philip wasn't interested in the crude. He just wanted to push his cart to the far end of the street where the women selling soap sat dozing. He had to replenish his stocks since a whole shelf in his shop had emptied as if by a miracle when some fools headed for a safari had dropped by.

This time the shadow appeared on the wall of a still-unfinished hotel that flanked the north side of the marketplace. It was high noon and ordinary shadows were hiding, crouching at people's feet, emerging only now and then to accompany their masters' languid movements. But the shadow on the wall was looming high above. It looked like a man wearing a misshapen animal mask with horns. It moved along the wall, as if observing the activity amid the market stalls from above.

Philip glanced at the people around him, but they all had other things on their mind. They stared down at the ground where they had laid out their wares, or streamed along the packed narrow streets. He gave a man walking in front of him a pat on the back and pointed to the shadow on the wall across the street. But the man just shook his head, baffled.

That day an oil tanker exploded at the market and several people were burnt to death. The papers said that the fuel had been ignited by a cigarette butt. As Philip was reading the newspaper report, a customer told him that a policeman had been strangled. He was found exactly on the day that Philip first spotted the shadow in front of his shop. Just a few streets down, in the bushes.

'Why on earth would anyone kill a uniformed policeman in broad daylight?' the outraged man in a pink jacket asked as he loaded his shopping into a carrier bag.

'That's really odd,' Philip replied absent-mindedly and once the customer was gone, pulled down the shutters on his shop. On his way home he guzzled down three 50-ml sachets of whisky. As he opened the door of his house, a chill ran down his body. He felt a draught rippling above his head and his cap flew out into the dust of the street. He set his bag down on the doorstep, then reached down for his cap, which lay crumpled in the shadow. Almost imperceptibly, the shadow changed shape and turned into a figure. He left his cap there and ran inside.

He slammed the door shut and bolted into the bathroom. He turned on the rusty shower with clumsy fingers and climbed under the weak stream of tepid water, shoes and all. Soon his shirt was soaking wet. He felt pressure on his chest and acid rushing from his stomach. He nearly choked on his own vomit, which spurted onto the walls in uncontrollable bursts. His stomach completely empty, he staggered back into the room and started rummaging around not knowing what he was looking for. He hurled a full bottle of beer against the shelf where he kept his accounts, knocked the table over and slumped down on his bed. A loudspeaker in the street started to play evening music. He lay there pinned to his bed by the rhythm of the makossa.

He had a dream in which he saw himself emerge from a corner and punch a running policeman in the face. He drags the unconscious policeman into a side street and tightens a chain around his neck. He kicks the man in the face until the back of his neck snaps. Next, he sees himself as he walks the length of the market, pushing a cart loaded with soap and boxes of soft drinks. Casually he flicks a cigarette butt towards a dark rivulet of oil running along the pavement. He doesn't look back but is aware of horrified screams, interrupted by a sudden explosion. He smiles and turns into a side street. He comes home and starts to tug at his sleeping self. 'Up you get! Time to go!'

Philip gets up. He pieces his dream together, fragment by tiny fragment. It was extremely vivid and clear, like watching a film. He throws a few things into a carrier bag. He wonders if the shadow presages future disasters, or if it appears at random. If it is warning him of something that is about to happen or suggests that very soon he . . . yes he . . . will do something. But it no longer matters.

He throws the bag across his shoulder and goes out of the house, leaving the door wide open. He has an inkling that he won't be coming back, but nevertheless does not leave behind anything important. He goes around the corner and knocks on the door of the police station. It is late, all the bosses have gone home. The guard takes him to a cell and leaves him there until the morning.

At sunrise he confesses to a sergeant that he had murdered the policeman and deliberately started the fire in which eight people died. There is nothing to investigate and Philip is soon taken to the prison in Douala. The prison where even rats rot away. He sees many pairs of suspicious eyes peering at him from the gloomy cell. He'll have a lot of explaining to do. But finally, at least, he won't need to be afraid of the shadow, of himself, or of the world around him.

He is happy to be here. He feels liberated. It doesn't matter in the least whether or not he really is a murderer.

THE NEW WORLD

A bunch of young locals crowded around him in the arrivals hall. They outshouted each other, ruthlessly pushing and shoving, bumping into him more than into one another. He retreated all the way to the wall, as far back as possible.

They'll collect his bags. They'll hail him a cab. They'll look after him. They'll show him around. They'll find him a beautiful and certifiably healthy girl. They're his friends. If he's brought any contraband, he needn't worry, they'll make the necessary arrangements. They'll find him a hotel room. Take him to the best restaurants. They'll chase muggers away. So how can they help him?

'I don't need anything, I'm not giving you anything—go away, beat it!' he muttered angrily and in desperation when they ignored his polite refusals. They kept pushing closer and closer. He felt their hot breath on his face. Sprays of saliva made his forehead and nose wet. He was drenched in sweat.

'Stop that right now! Leave me the fuck alone!' he shrieked in a falsetto in his own language to make sure nobody understood. His cracked, high-pitched voice had the desired effect. Those closest to him took half a step back. But they hadn't quite given up. They just recoiled in surprise. After a moment's silence and an exchange of stunned looks, they started pushing and shoving him again and repeating their offers. Ernest could barely take a deep breath as he kept one hand on the money belt with his passport and protected his face from the attackers' wild gesticulations with the other.

I can give you a lift into town. You'll be safe with me. I know all the cops. I'll take you on safari. I can sell you genuine masks. Very cheap. I'll help you through customs.

'Noooo!' Ernest screamed again, his voice rising even higher. Helpless and purple with rage, he pulled out all the stops. He was shaken by a fit of coughing. The porters took a discreet step back and this time Ernest took advantage of the moment of surprise. Arms flailing frantically, with the heroic effort of a deranged epileptic he broke through the cordon. He headed straight for the conveyor belt where his luggage was supposed to arrive. The swarm of helpers trailed behind him like a conga line at a party.

His suitcase arrived in under an hour. By then Ernest had swallowed a handful of pills. Nevertheless, he was still incandescent with rage, which kept even the boldest of would-be helpers at a respectful distance of at least a metre. As soon as he spotted his expensive Samsonite, he lunged at it and clutched it to his chest.

A man in a suit and a pair of dark glasses emerged from the crowd of porters. He gave Ernest a nice smile and offered to help. There would be no problems, he knew what to do, and would sort everything out for his new master. Ernest was about to swear at him but instead just bit his lip, glowered, and headed towards customs without saying a word. The man seemed amused and just shook his head as he lit a cigarette.

A few minutes later Ernest was disgorging the contents of his luggage onto the counter. The man in glasses watched as he spread out on the rickety table his underwear, the creased shirts he'd have to have ironed as soon as he got to the hotel, books, marketing manuals and a bottle of brandy. He did everything slowly, mechanically, with resignation. Maybe the pills had kicked in, maybe he was acclimatizing. What mattered was that he had freed himself of the porters' clutches. He took out everything, down to the last pencil. The customs official carefully examined each object from every side and pondered every worn sock. Then he proposed five dollars as customs duty for the bottle of brandy. Reluctantly, Ernest handed over a banknote and after another 15-minute wait for a stamped customs declaration he crammed his stuff back into the suitcase and left the terminal.

Outside he was hit by a wall of scorching heat. A throng of taxi drivers leapt at his bags. He resisted at first but then a guy in a basketball T-shirt snatched the Samsonite out of his hand and made a dash for a rusty Toyota. Ernest ran after him and kicked him in the rear. The pack of taxi drivers burst out laughing. The men looked on in amusement as he pushed his way through the taxis, gasping, to the other side of the road, heading for the first normal taxi driver at this airport who didn't leap at him like a monkey!

'Rue Franceville, s'il vous plaît,' he said, and the car glided off quietly.

At last he had got out of that madhouse. A lucky escape. They could have robbed him without him even noticing. Every single one of them looked like a thief. It's best to rely only on yourself. Be confident and arrogant, that's what shuts them up.

Palm trees raced past the car windows in the scorching heat, and he wondered what kind of dump he'd landed in. Of his own free will. Oh well, he'd manage somehow. Hopefully the firm would look after him. They'd provide him with a car and a driver and a decent air-conditioned apartment. And tomorrow he'd kill the guy who was supposed to meet him.

They drove for over half an hour, but the town centre was still nowhere to be seen. They meandered down an asphalt road, past tall cranes in the harbour.

'Are we nearly there?' he asked impatiently.

'Yes, we're nearly there,' the driver muttered. He turned into the nearest street and pulled up next to some kind of a warehouse built of corrugated iron.

'Is this Franceville?'

The question froze on Ernest's lips when he saw a bunch of men in torn T-shirts come out of the warehouse and approach him at a leisurely gait. The taxi driver smiled at him in the rear-view mirror.

'You'd better leave your stuff and your wallet here and continue on foot. You're almost there now.'

UNDER A SUNLIT SKY

I knew it was time to get out of this place. The only thing keeping me here was my dog, but I was able to take him along. Only Jacob and me, wouldn't that be something! I didn't care whether we found anything to eat. It made no difference. He would always find something. A bone, a fly, the odd ant. And as for myself, I don't eat much. A few peanuts and some wild fruit will do me fine. We'll set out on a long journey and be the envy of all my schoolmates. I couldn't care less about the fellow everyone else in our compound calls Father. He'll be amazed to learn that we made it to town! I will make some money at last and be able to go to a proper school. I will train Jacob and he'll help me when we're living in town. He can catch thieves or look for lost property. People keep losing things. We'll take care of ourselves and have a good life.

So what's keeping me here? Maybe the candlelight I see at bedtime. Or the view of the sky just before nightfall when I sit on top of the hill. I've been more or less driven out. It's not the beatings, it's the way they look at me that makes it clear they don't want me around.

All I need to do is wait for the rainy season to end. Wait for the day. Then I'll stand on my own two feet. How will the sky look in that place so far away?

It was early morning by the time we reached town and the sky had only just begun to take on a tinge of colour. On the outskirts I could make out some figures in the fog. A bunch of boys, around my age, at the crossroads. All I could see in the glare of the morning sun were their outlines. I quickened my pace but they started running towards me. Before I could duck, a stone whooshed past my head. It was too late to do anything. I heard a scream and hit the ground. I got kicked in the ribs several times. There was some laughter, followed by silence.

Nothing happened for a long time before I dared raise my head. There was no one around and my dog was also gone. 'Jacob!' I shouted desperately, scurrying from one side of the road to the other. Then I heard some whining from a ditch. The dog had a wound under one eye that was bleeding and couldn't get up on his legs. I picked him up. He nuzzled against my shoulder. He was shivering and his panting alternated with a soft, despairing wail.

I started walking down a street. My head felt empty. I couldn't think and I was barely aware of where I was going.

Suddenly a figure loomed up before me. I nearly crashed into him. I steadied myself and retreated in fright. I saw an old man with a white beard giving me a stern look. Wordlessly he gestured for me to follow him into a courtyard. Past caring, I was too weak to run or resist.

I fell on my knees in the shade of a palm tree. The old man laid the dog down in the grass and disappeared. Soon he was back with a small bundle of longish leaves on a tray encrusted with painted stones and shells. These were all things I'd been told to steer clear of back home. One day we'd come across a small shrine covered with the same kind of stones on our way to the fields and old Yata, who was looking after us, chased us away with frenzied shouting and prayers. I was never allowed to go anywhere near the herbalist's hut at the far end of our village. To me he embodied everything that was mysterious and terrifying about the world, and to catch even a fleeting glimpse of it could prove fatal for a child.

The old man cleaned out Jacob's wounds with water and covered them with some leaves he had ground up in a mortar. I held them down, stroking his wet fur. After a while I felt his shivers subside. The old man washed his hands and poured himself a glass of palm wine. Then he slumped down into a wicker chair and stared at me without saying a word. He was waiting for me to say something. I decided to tell him my story. All about my journey. All about my mother and about Jacob.

I broke down before finishing the first sentence.

The old man brought a deckchair, put it under the palm tree and I collapsed into it, sobbing. I don't know how long I lay there. All I remember is being angry with myself. I was doing my best not to lose control, but failing miserably. I had set out for the city to take care of myself. To prove to all and sundry that I was no longer a little boy. That I could stand up for myself without being a burden to anyone. And now I couldn't even hold back my tears.

I wept for being so weak.

I buried Jacob's body at the end of the old man's garden. The freshly dug grave was immediately drenched by a shower of rain.

I spent the night in the hallway. I slept like a log, without dreaming. In the morning, the old man shook my hand by way of goodbye and made a mark on my forehead with his thumb. I thanked him, although I knew I no longer needed any protection.

I found myself back in the rainy streets filled with mud and the pungent stench of blocked sewers. In desperation, the idea of going back home flashed through my mind. But I rejected the temptation.

All I'd eaten for several days now were some kola nuts and a mango. I had a few sips of the old man's palm wine but it didn't agree with me. My stomach rumbled loudly and felt like it was tied in knots. I quickly dived into a side street and squatted down behind a pile of rubbish. Just then a boy came around the corner. As he spotted me, he gave a whistle and slowed down. 'Oh-la-la, what have we got here?' he croaked and took a catapult out of his pocket. In my mind I replayed the laugh I heard a day before. The flash of lightning, the flame of fury in his eyes and the pain in my chest. It must have been one of the boys from the gang who'd set upon me on the outskirts of town. Crouched awkwardly with my trousers down I waited for the blow, paralysed.

The boy bent down to pick up a rock and without taking his eyes off me yelled something about bastards that muck up his street. He shot his catapult, the rock whooshed and bounced off into a puddle to one side. He took aim again but was stopped by the sound of ear-piercing barking. Unnerved, he looked around, since there was no sign of a dog. He surveyed the hedge and checked every path leading to the nearest crossroads. Then came a low growling and the poor sod took to his heels. After just a few metres he began to scream as the T-shirt covering his groin ripped apart, revealing a fresh wound. He fell down and picked himself up repeatedly before vanishing behind a fence.

Eventually I managed to regain control of my emotions and pull up my trousers. Something invisible brushed against my legs. It was Jacob. I could feel his breath and smell. I knew it was him.

I knew my only friend wouldn't desert me! He had stayed with me and was now looking out for me. It was as if I had woken from a dream. Recuperated, I felt ready to start afresh.

I went to the car park next to the bus station. The place was teeming with people. They were lugging enormous parcels for their journey, shouting, and trying to squeeze onto crowded bush taxis, happily exchanging greetings with neighbours from their villages and praising each other's purchases in the market. This was the world I had dreamt of. The promise of new friends and experiences. The station was my biggest opportunity and I had to seize it. I decided to stay there until I found some decent work. This was where I was going to launch my career.

I was sitting on the low wall in front of a bar listening to snippets of conversation. The bar belonged to Madam Buke. She was skipping about in a brightly coloured dress that was pristine even though she was handling gravy and dirty dishes all day long. She was a big woman, weighing at least 100 kilos, yet her breasts didn't stick out like those of the women in my village but merged with her belly into a single enormous mass under her dress. I was awestruck.

As Madam Buke ladled groundnut pap into her customers' bowls, I stared at her hands smeared with the grey substance. I hesitated for a moment. Her hands seemed familiar, though I couldn't work out why. It was uncanny. There was something almost intimately familiar not just about the bulging veins on her hands but also the way she picked up the bowls and served her customers. I was fascinated by this mystery and that is why I didn't do a runner after the first day, weary as I was and barely able stand on my feet. Is this woman someone close to me? Or was this just a portent of the fate that someone had preordained for me?

My gawping must have been all too obvious, for she noticed me straight away. I told her I wanted to work for her and without further ado, she ushered me into the courtyard. There were two big water bowls and a smaller one for kitchen waste. I felt as if I was in paradise. I'd make the odd coin or two and anything left over would feed me and my dog.

Things didn't turn out quite as straightforward as that. The customers' plates came back almost empty, gnawed down to the last chicken bone. All that was left over were some nibbled stones from shea fruit or stringy scraps of tough meat of uncertain origin. But even that was better than nothing. I would drop some on the ground and Jacob would gulp it all down in seconds. The meat disappeared without a trace.

But the next day around lunchtime Madam Buke stomped up to me fuming and yelling that I'd gobbled up a chicken leg she'd cooked for a guest. Clean off the plate. 'Who do you think you are! That wasn't our deal! If it ever happens again, I'll roast you alive!'

I would never dare do anything like that. But I had my suspicions as to who the culprit was. 'Jacob! You mustn't do that!' I shouted when I was sure I was alone in the courtyard. Jacob leapt towards me with an apologetic whimper. On the third day, as I was happily washing the dishes, the door suddenly flew open. Madam Buke burst in and slapped me across the face so hard that I fell to the ground. That was the end of my career at her establishment.

I put it down to work experience. I hadn't made a single franc but at least now I knew how to fight for my wages. I had to keep going, there was no other way. Keep trying in another street, another neighbourhood. I've been in this town for a year now. I've peeled yams, washed bowls and cutlery, roasted and sold corn on the cob. I never made any money but I've had enough to eat. I've done everything grown-ups do. And that's how I've became one as well.

But I have kept looking. I couldn't believe this was all there was to it.

One Saturday Jacob and I went for a walk and came upon an old man sitting on the shore, looking out to sea. Though he wasn't actually looking, as he was blind. He was just happy to be breathing in the smell of the sea and of fish bones again. He had grown up on the beaches of Kribi and used to push a cart of roasted fish up and down the streets until one day he got into a fight with another man, whose head he smashed in. Nothing serious, just a minor concussion needing a stitch or two, but the man's father happened to be a big shot in a suit. The old man ended up in a prison in Douala. The worst prison in the country, where even the rats come to a bad end.

'A human being is more than just head and flesh and bones. You can't imprison a soul in a cage,' he said, nodding as if agreeing with himself. We chatted for a while. Neither of us had anything to do and we just sat there chilling. He told me about the time he'd had nothing to eat. They didn't feed him and he couldn't even afford to buy some cassava or a couple of bananas. 'For everyone else the day has two halves—day and night. It's something they never think to question. But for me the day lasted only for an hour or two. Sometimes not even that. Sometimes it was night all day long. And by the time I was due for release, I'd fallen ill and lost my sight.'

The man spent the whole day walking up and down the port, his face turned to the waves breaking on the shore in the strong wind. He asked me if the sea in these parts was as infinite as in Kribi, where he came from. If everything was as pristine and calm as far as the eye could see, all the way to the point where the blue water met the blue sky.

I told him that this was exactly what the sea was like here. That as far as the eye could see, there was nothing but a vast body of water and all that was visible in the distance was a flat blue surface with the hat of the sun disappearing slowly on the horizon.

It wasn't true, of course. In the distance, huge oil derricks jutted out of the water and three tankers lay at anchor on the horizon. And the sea was steely grey, gloomy and sinister. The clouds were piling up, ready to crush us all to the ground.

MR HAT

Everyone in town called him Mr Hat. The hat seemed to have merged with his curly grey hair—no one had ever seen him without it. It was an enormous old hat, made of leather and all crumpled. Greasy, sweaty and covered in stains of mysterious origin. He never took it off, not even in the scorching sun or a sweltering bar. He must have worn it even while he slept or got washed.

As soon as he set foot in a fresh watering hole, people would fall silent and give him a respectful nod. He would stand in the doorway without a word and wait for the customers to move aside and let him through. Then he would turn to the barmaid: 'A beer, madam,' and solemnly take a seat on a bench. He would wiggle about to gain more space for himself and then sit in silence, watching the customers who had by now resumed their conversations. He would sip his beer straight from the bottle and then turn to one of the men in the bar.

'You're in big trouble with your back, my friend,' he said, opening a small bag with some purple bulbs. He sliced off a bit of a bulb and used the hard end of the tuber to rub the man's lower back. The man stuck his back out obediently and bent down, moaning as the stinging pain drove the ailment out of his body.

Mr Hat would then quickly finish off his beer, collect his bits and pieces and shuffle out into the busy street. He wasn't one for long conversations and if someone asked him a question, he'd just give a pensive nod or offer a vague general reply. People say he could always guess what was ailing them or was about to afflict them. No one protested if Mr Hat said: 'Your joints are all fucked up, let me take a look' or 'Your ticker is about to peg out, you'll snuff it soon unless you take the brew I'm about to mix for you.' Everyone gratefully did as they were told: conversations would stop and street vendors would park their handcarts, readily take off their clothes in the middle of a crowd and let Mr Hat check them out, feel them up and apply his ointments. He never wanted any payment except for a token small coin, a beer or a bowl of rice. As he walked, the tiny 10-franc coins would tinkle in the bag tied to his waist. And even though they were the smallest and thinnest aluminium coins, the bag was always bulging. It was proof of his status and success.

Sometimes I would spot him in our street too. He would saunter down the middle of the road with a slow, rolling gait, paying no attention to the traffic. Instead of hooting their horns at full blast as they usually did, drivers would wait patiently until there was enough room between the potholes for them to drive around him. You would often see the huge hat on his head rising up above a tangled cluster of taxis. He paid them no heed although he could feel them staring at his back. From a distance he looked as if he never turned his head, but I could see him casting glances all around even when his eyes seemed fixed on the ground. He had the whole town under his spell.

One day I was sitting at the Horse Bar, people-watching. I watched his every move for an infuriatingly long time, waiting for him to notice me. I was fiddling with a now-empty bottle of Fanta with one hand, while the other clutched a 10-franc coin I'd swiped from my mum's drawer. These coins had become a rarity and had not been accepted in shops for a long time now. Their only use was as symbolic reward for healers, as no spell would work without them.

Mr Hat stood with his head in profile to me. He seemed to have registered my presence but wouldn't turn in my direction. He picked a man standing at the bar, gave him some herbs and explained how to use them to get rid of a bowel problem. I've never figured out how he chose his customers. How he knew that they had some problem. And I couldn't understand why he wouldn't pay any attention to me.

The two men patted each other on the back, Mr Hat collected his gear and headed out of the bar, past my table. I stopped him at the door. I couldn't bear to wait any longer. I reached out my hand with the coin and gave him an imploring look. Mr Hat sized me up with a poker face. Then he put his things down and took out a small, well-worn box full of a dark red ointment. He smeared some over my temples and chest.

'The fever will be gone by tomorrow,' he said, and my coin rattled as it fell into the bag to join hundreds of others. He was gone before I had time to say thank you.

After he left my whole body seemed to be on fire. His ointment left an unbearable burning sensation wherever it was applied. With clenched teeth I took comfort in the thought that I would be better once I got over the initial pain. It was the forces of good and evil fighting inside my body. I was a man, after all.

The next day a nasty rash appeared in every spot the man had touched. The burning sensation slowly faded but the tiny rash that remained was dreadfully itchy. And my temperature refused to subside. On the contrary—I was so weakened by a raging fever alternating with shivers that I couldn't get out of bed. When my father came back from work that night, he knew immediately that I'd contracted malaria again. He rushed to a neighbour to borrow some money. They shouted at each other for a while then made up again. A week later I was fine. I still have light patches on my skin from Mr Hat's ointment.

A NEW JOB

I can hardly remember how many days, weeks or months have passed since I last had a job. Not that the last was particularly exciting, and it wasn't well paid either. Or rather, I wasn't paid at all, I survived on the small tips guests slipped into my pocket as a reward for my services. But I can't complain.

From morning till night, I would stand by the door of the Akwa Hotel. I would push the door open and carry the guests' luggage. I wore a smart red uniform, with a cap and gloves. I would walk proudly up and down, smile at the frowning businessmen who came for meetings in the hotel bar and go out onto the pavement to greet the ladies. I would give the hotel guests directions, hail them a cab, fix them up with money changers. I'd receive a coin here and a couple there. People never spend more than they need to. Including the richest men in the country. But when I emptied my pockets in the evening, there would always be enough cash for a beer and a small roasted fish. Compared to other people in my street I was living a life of luxury.

But one night there was a problem. A young woman in a red minidress got out of a taxi. Seductively swaying hips, deep cleavage, gleaming lipgloss and a curiously large wig; in a word, a prostitute. I was on strict instructions from the hotel manager not to admit this kind of woman into the lobby or the restaurant. Ours was a decent establishment, and my job was to keep order. I stopped her in the doorway and said politely: 'Miss, you're not allowed in here. You must have got the wrong address.' She snapped at me, tried to force her way in and threw a tantrum. But rules are rules. Eventually a man came over from reception, apologized to her and slapped me across the face. I didn't understand until he returned and said that she was a government minister's daughter. Next day I was out on my ear.

I spent days trudging around every business in the neighbourhood—restaurants, shops, warehouses, repair shops, stations, supermarkets. None had any vacancies, not even the lowliest of the low. Eventually my despair turned into total apathy. The days flowed through my fingers. The only thing I had to eat was fruit thrown away at the market. I couldn't pay my rent and started sleeping rough under the bridge. Until one day . . .

I was sitting by the river when my view was blocked by a stocky figure. It was a White man. He wanted to know the way from Deido to the port. I explained and he sat down next to me. He offered me some biscuits and produced a bottle of pastis. It was the best drink I've ever tasted. He also gave me cigarettes, the most expensive kind, American. We talked. He asked all sorts of questions: which neighbourhoods were safe and which were not, where the good eateries were, how much he should expect to pay for things without being ripped off, where you can get cheap souvenirs to take back to Europe and so on. He was new to our neck of the woods.

I sipped the pastis and chatted, feeling better than I had in a long time. It occurred to me that I could offer to help. I could be his guide, and he could pay me in food and drink. But I didn't dare suggest it, knowing how I looked—dirty, ragged.

When we were about halfway through the bottle and had each smoked five cigarettes, he turned to me and looked me in the eye. Then he proposed something that made my head spin. He needed someone to watch over his house, look after the household and the garden. I could start next week, as soon as he had sorted out all the paperwork and moved from the hotel to the house. He couldn't pay me much to begin with, but I wouldn't live in poverty. I would get 50,000 and he'd pay more if I did well.

I stared at him, perplexed. To convince me, he gave me a 10,000 note by way of a deposit. 10,000 was as much as I had earned in 10 days in the best of times. Dumbfounded, I was momentarily at a loss for words.

'But this, this, this . . . is uncanny!' I shouted happily. 'I must be dreaming!'

'Now you've really screwed up, man,' said the White man in dismay and vanished into thin air.

THE SNAKE MAN
AND THE LION WOMAN

Returning to Ebolowa along a familiar route I spotted a curious clay hut under the waterfall, one I had not seen there before. The reason I hadn't noticed it was because it hadn't been there. The structure was unusually large by local standards and it caught my attention when I spotted it out of the window of the van. After driving another kilometre, I decided to get off. I tapped the driver on his cap, and he stepped on the brakes, sending backpacks flying off the car roof. He couldn't understand why I was getting off halfway along the trip for which I'd paid him 3,000 francs. Without saying a word he watched me clamber up to the roof to collect my bag. The locals are not interested in waterfalls and things like that. The dusty road ahead of me, lined with banana trees, looked pleasant enough. Thirty minutes later I found myself at the waterfall.

On the roof of the hut small pennants with brewery logos wafted in the breeze and a puzzled, faded face stared down at me from an old poster on the wall. It showed a grey-haired man with his arms in the air and despair in his eyes. Above the face I could make out a text in huge letters that read 'What's eating you is under your clothes!'

It was an advert for a spray against lice, fleas and other creepy-crawlies. What struck me was that although I was positive that the hut had not been there a week ago, it looked quite old. The poster showed evidence of years of exposure to the sun, while the humidity had split and softened the wood of the boards, the terrace and the door . . . I didn't know what made me get off the van, or what it was about the house that captivated me enough to make me break my journey even though another ride would not be available for ages, if at all. I had no idea if more than one bush taxi a day went to Ebolowa, nor what I wanted to, or was supposed to, see in this house. Had I not been quite convinced that only a week ago all there was to be seen under the waterfall were a few weeds, there would have been nothing to distinguish this hut from thousands of others that I passed every day and barely noticed. Anyone else would probably have thought there was nothing unusual about the place.

But I felt like a character in a dream who is seeing himself from somewhere far above. Everything shimmered in the scorching heat and all the sounds reaching me seemed to be muffled. Everything seemed to happen in a matter of seconds.

With a frown on his face, the bartender served a hairy woman. He brought her a pitcher of palm wine, a bowl filled with green liquid in which there floated a chunk of meat the size of an antelope thigh and a portion of fufu as big as someone's head. The woman threw herself on the meat as if it was the first meal of her life. Only then did I notice her golden-yellow eyes and enormous canines sticking out of her moustachioed lips. She was a lion woman.

The grumpy bartender slammed down a bottle of beer in front of me without a word. When I asked how long the bar had been here, he just muttered that it had always been here and disappeared into a dark cubbyhole. Apart from me and the lion woman there were only a few people on the terrace, not the kind I usually meet. A man sat on the low fence chewing cola nuts with a young black mamba coiled around his neck. He stared at the churning waves that formed a white fog on the surface of the water. His face, belly and arms were covered in long scars and he had a small cart from which he sold herbs for snake venom. You have to keep chewing one of these herbs until it fills your mouth, then suck the venom out of the wound. It will be absorbed by the herbal pulp, which you have to spit out quickly and then sprinkle the wound with this ground black rock. It's a special kind of coal with absorbent qualities, he said. Then you mix some other herbs with quicklime and a drop of palm oil, and apply the mixture to the skin, massaging it in for hours on end. This will save the life even of someone bitten by a mamba. The bar owner shook his head as he listened to the scarred man's explanations and pretended to be annoyed by his sales pitch. There were lots of snakes living beneath the waterfall but nothing like that had ever happened to him, he'd never needed any of this stuff. And why should he believe the man anyway? He should first demonstrate that his herbs really work. The scarred man looked helpless for a moment. Then he finished his drink, uncoiled the mamba from around his neck, opened his eyes wide so that they were popping out and started panting to provoke the mamba into biting his lower arm. The languid mamba stirred sleepily in his hands. The bar owner mocked the man, saying the snake was about to bite the dust: he must have pulled its teeth out, or maybe the mamba hadn't yet managed to produce fresh venom after biting some animal. As he said that, the snake stirred, shook its tail (or rather, one end of its body, as snakes don't have tails) and in a flash, plunged its needle-sharp teeth into the man's elbow, going straight for the vein. The scarred man juddered and froze. The mamba held its grip on his arm for a while, then dropped to the ground and slithered into the shade under the herb cart.

Everyone around stopped talking and stared, astounded, as white foam started to pour out of the trembling man's mouth and he collapsed onto the ground. Several of us ran up to him and it was immediately obvious that he wasn't faking it, he had really suffered a serious bite. We looked at the cart piled high with all sorts of herbs, bits of bark and some pieces of black stone. The bar owner hadn't fully taken in the snake man's explanations so we weren't sure what to do first. While we rummaged through the herbs, the hairy lion woman elbowed her way towards us, pushed the bar owner aside, gave a loud burp, and sank her teeth so hard into the poor man's hand that she nearly bit half of it clean off. She began to suck out the wound. Sweating profusely, she spat out the blood as she sucked it out. Then she picked up a rock and ground one of the black stones into a fine powder which she sprinkled on the wound. Without a word, she picked up the snake man in her hairy, long-clawed arms, put him in his cart which she pushed over to a hut behind the bushes where she lived. Whether she healed him or ate him I never discovered.

THE FIELD

A goat and a tiny patch of a field were his only possessions. Cassava, groundnuts, tomatoes and plantains: that was all he ever needed. He never tried to sell any of his crops at the market. If he harvested more than he needed, he would swap a bunch of plantains with a neighbour for a bag of salt or a small barrel of palm wine. He had never made as much as a single franc at the market. He had never had a job and never heard the word 'pension'. One day, when the village chief showed him a piece of paper with some scribbles and a picture of some old building on it, he studied it with a deadpan face and gave it back. He couldn't understand why he should exchange vitally important things for scraps of paper. He saw no reason to sell his labour, himself or his family's honour.

Then a few townspeople arrived. In exchange for his tiny field they offered him 100,000 francs together with another, even smaller field nearby. 'You'll just work the land and in a year's time it will yield the same crops, if not more. And you'll have 100,000 on top!'

A hundred thousand scraps of paper! What's the world come to! He tossed the wad of banknotes under their feet and said no. Then excavators arrived and he lay down among the cassava bushes. He settled down comfortably in a ditch waiting for the machine to pound him into the ground. If they wanted to take his field, they'd have to take his skeleton as well. Two men in uniforms slapped him around and easily dragged him back to his hut. He resisted as best he could, wresting himself free of their clutches and throwing himself on the ground, but his aged body was too weak for the builders' muscles.

Before long, a furrow was dug across his field, marking out a new road that was to connect the capital with the oil fields in the north. As the steamrollers stamped down the laterite, he saw the earth bleed. After a while, the building work was halted for lack of money. The only thing that remained was the deep, silent furrow lined with mounds of dug-up clay on both sides.

Eventually his neighbour persuaded him to go and take a look at the site of his new field. He surveyed the small patch of rocky earth, covered in shrubs and thorny weeds, and what he saw confirmed what he had suspected all along. He no longer had the strength to start again from scratch. And certainly not here, in this spot. He returned to his hut and took out a handful of banknotes from the drawer. He scattered them on the floor and watched as the breeze played with them. Then he picked them up and stuffed some into his pocket. He knew that he had lost. Tears of humiliation welled up in his eyes.

He would go on a bender, buying the most expensive drink there was.

WHO'S THAT BRAWLING
ANYWAY?

Tamba dropped his axe, set down the bowl he'd been carrying on his head and unloaded the logs, putting them down by the door. He held his head under the pump and splashed lukewarm water over it. He was ready to begin.

The other night he had gone to a bar feeling desperate and sat there drinking the cheapest palm wine. As usual, he listened to the chatter of the old men who had nothing to do. Out of sheer boredom, he mindlessly chiselled away with a knife at the old bench he was sitting on. When he paid his bill, the bar owner saw what he had done and started to swear at the top of his voice. He was about to charge Tamba for the piece of cracked old wood but after taking a better look he declared that the wine was on the house and even poured him one for the road. He grabbed the bench, smashed it against the floor, breaking off its rickety legs and proudly propped what was left of it against the bar counter. Everyone could now admire the face of a small deity covered in old grease stains and winking mischievously at its new victims. Everyone thought that its facial expression had been captured perfectly, fittingly and convincingly.

'Hey, Tamba, you could make a living doing this,' people said, giving him encouraging thumps on the back.

Tamba just stood there gobsmacked, staring at his handi-
work. After a while he let himself be persuaded. When inspected
carefully and from the right angle, the carved lines formed a face
that seemed to emerge from the surface as if trying to say something. This sort of thing would fetch good money at the market.
All he had to do was work it a little more delicately, stain it, give
it a lick of paint to tart it up a bit so that it appealed to foreigners.

The next day he was woken by loud banging on his door. A
man in a long tunic of the finest material stood in the yard.

'I heard you make masks. And very nice masks, too!' he said
by way of greeting.

Tamba remembered what had happened in the bar and was
relieved. He replied with a smile: 'Oh, no. Me and masks?! There
must be some misunderstanding.'

But the man went on undeterred: 'You're no good at lying.
You make masks under the direct protection of the gods. I
dropped by the bar this morning. I took one look and could tell
straight away.' The man's voice was deep and sombre. Tamba
tried to protest but words failed him. Beads of sweat formed on
his forehead. The man kept talking but Tamba wasn't listening.
He was trying to make sense of what had happened. Last night
in the bar must have been a sign. He wondered if he should take
on this new role. Slowly, his mind came back to the man in the
expensive tunic. But once he heard how much he could get for
making a mask, the deal was done.

Today Tamba is a new man. Gone are the days of hanging
around with no hope. That face didn't emerge from the wood by
accident. It's a gift from the gods. He just can't understand why
it took so long to make itself known. With the money he can get

for a single mask he could have been living a life of leisure, had his house fixed, eaten out and bought new clothes whenever he felt like it.

First thing the next morning he headed for the forest to forage for the right kind of wood. It had to be light enough to sink a knife into but also firm enough not to break. It should be durable so that it didn't crack after a few rainy days, but also supple so that the seller could make it look 'ancient'. A mask must look old, that's what gives it its market value.

He shook his head to sprinkle some water from his hair onto the pieces of wood he had propped up against the wall. He picked them up one by one, feeling their weight in his hands and examining them. He talked to them. He spoke to them the way he did to his mates in the street when they were dreaming up some dangerous piece of mischief. 'You up for it, fellas? Anyone scared shitless? Nah, we can do it. We can do it, but you've got to help me. We must stick together.'

He picked a medium-sized piece and ran his knife over it lightly to see how supple it was. His uncertainty melted away after just a few strokes. But the material wasn't shaping up as needed. It was one thing to sit drinking palm wine while scratching at the bench without thinking about it, and quite another trying to focus and capture a specific shape and geometry of lines. After an hour's work he put the piece of wood down in the doorway and took a few steps back. He could see straight away that it wasn't any good. The face was lacking a lively expression and many of the incisions were clustered in a tangle of lines that resembled the same words again and again, written on a sheet of paper with a broken biro.

'Hmm, this is not going to be easy,' Tamba said to himself. He lit a cigarette and doubts started to creep in as the smoke rose to the sky. He spent the rest of the day sitting under the roof staring at the first mask. Then he went to a street stall, knocked back a whole demijohn of palm wine and went home to sleep.

Next morning he inspected the fruit of his work again. Nobody would buy this. At that moment a fresh gust of wind blew from the thicket. The masters of the forest were shaking him awake. He had to start from scratch. His hands trembled and he felt the blood coursing feverishly in his veins.

After preparing its surface with a machete he plunged the knife into a new piece of wood. This time it felt quite different from the previous day. Everything went smoothly and naturally, as if he'd been doing this all his life. The blade glided with certainty, the incisions were precise and the outlines accurate. He didn't stop to think who the mask would represent, he just knew that he'd be happy with the result. He was quite sure of that. The knife darted nimbly to and fro between his fingers and a face was emerging rapidly. Now he just had to give it a final clean and blow away any dirt. A single cursory glance told him that this was indeed it. He set the mask aside, stuck a cigarette in his mouth and immediately started working on another piece of wood.

He worked all day except when he had to dash to the well for a drink of water. And one more day he worked, and another. His hand moved automatically, he was in a trance, so oblivious to the world around him that he didn't notice a gaping wound in his left thumb and the blood pouring into the freshly carved incisions. He used up all the wood he had brought back after praying in the forest. The masks stood lined up on the doorstep, from the smallest to the largest, propped up against the clay wall. He exhaled deeply and examined them joyfully. He recognized fertility fetishes, masks for healing the blind, funereal statuettes, animal totems and various protective amulets. Tamba thought they were magnificent and it made him as happy as a lark. All that was left to do was sprinkle some woodworm powder on the masks and smear them with grease or palm oil.

A few days later the buyer arrived. As he entered Tamba's courtyard, he spotted the huge number of masks ready to be exhibited and his eyes lit up. He approached slowly and picked up the first item admiringly. A fine piece work. He gave a smile but then shuddered and quickly put the statuette back. He didn't even touch any of the others and just walked around, before slowly retreating. He shook his head in puzzlement and cast a furious glance at the surprised Tamba, then lowered his gaze as if something inside him had broken. Knees trembling, he headed for the gate and disappeared without a word.

Tamba wanted to chase after him but he was so shocked that he couldn't move. This was to be his big day, he was going to make enough money to keep him going for months. But instead the buyer had run off in a fright, leaving him alone with perfectly executed masks that not even the best shaman from Foumban would be ashamed of. Disappointed, he gathered up his treasures and carried them to the storeroom.

He popped out to buy supplies of alcohol and, once home, got drunk on his own.

From then on, he left his hut more and more rarely. He vanished from the streets and the tradespeople gradually forgot about him. Only an old neighbour who had nothing better to do would sometimes mention him over a beer, when she shared the latest gossip from the street.

'Tamba seems to have a screw loose these days. He yells every night and beats his wife.'

'Nonsense. It's she who's beating him. I heard it. It was Tamba howling in pain.'

'You've both taken leave of your senses. Tamba has no wife. No one's ever seen her. Or maybe you have?'

'So why are they brawling every night? And who is that brawling anyway?'

I'M A BOY FROM A BOOK

I wasn't born like other children. The people in my street say I came into this world from a book. That's why I don't have a mother. That would explain it. One day I was sitting in the yard looking at Uncle smoking his pipe in the shade of a mango tree. He beckoned to me, so I plucked up the courage to move and sit closer to him. We started chatting, and that's when he told me the whole story. He said I didn't have a mother or a father and that one day I was blown here by the sea breeze along with the other pages that had been torn from a book. That's how it happened.

On the day I showed up in this town, the main street was carpeted with sheets of paper. These were pages ripped from books fluttering in the air. They got caught in the branches of trees, bedecking them like strange headless birds. The air was thick with smoke.

No one in this town knew me, and I roved the narrow alleyways in search of a woman who might take me in her arms. She'd be running up and down the streets until she saw me standing there helplessly amid all the commotion. She would call out my name, and I would throw my arms around her. I gazed deep into the faces of women I saw, in the hope of finding the one I might belong to. I wandered around the empty marketplace watching the burning leaves floating high above my head. The wind played havoc with them as it gusted at the billowing flames that turned them into a feathery black nothingness. The charred tatters disintegrated into minute particles and stung my eyes. In the Akwa neighbourhood angry locals had driven out the White people and razed their library to the ground. They flung all the books and files on the pavement, then tore them up, one by one, before setting fire to them on a pile of old tyres.

In the evening I found myself not far from a restaurant called The Mulet. To give my sore feet a break, I sat down on the bank of a canal. That's when Uncle Mongo called out to me and shared some of his roast fish—at least that's what he told me later. He was the first person I got to talk to in Douala. I told him that I didn't know anyone in this town and was looking for my parents. I couldn't remember anything and didn't know how I came to end up there. He didn't either, nor did anyone else in this street or in the neighbourhood. I was the boy who came into this world from one of the books drifting in the air that day.

Then Uncle Mongo took me to the woman who was to be my Auntie. She was in the restaurant kitchen, sitting amid her cooking pots, cleaning a huge barracuda. I stopped in the doorway while Uncle went up to her and mumbled something under his breath. She threw her hands up in the air and exclaimed: 'Holy Mother of God'.

She gave me a glass of water and I gulped it down—then a second, a third and a fourth. I was thirsty, having never tasted water before. I loved it. She asked how old I was but I just stared at her, not sure what she meant. She went to get a blanket, setting it down on the floor behind a cupboard with pots. I wrapped myself in it and tried to fall asleep. I lay awake till late at night listening to the sounds from the kitchen. I heard the scraping of a knife and the distant laughter of drunken customers out in the street, regularly interrupted by Auntie swearing in a dialect neither I nor the fish awaiting the pan could understand. Just like me, the fish lay there silent and still, its eyes set on the ceiling.

The next morning I woke up with the feeling that someone was watching me. I opened my eyes a tiny crack to look around without being noticed. Auntie was looming above me, sizing me up with a blank, inscrutable gaze. I wanted to wait for her to go out into the garden before getting up but she just stood there as if rooted to the spot. This went on for what seemed like an eternity and I was desperate to go to the toilet. It must have been all that water I had drunk. Yawning, I blinked sleepily.

'We get up earlier around here, my boy! Come on, go, get washed and I'll find you something nice to eat.'

From that day on, my name was Myboy.

Every morning Auntie and I would go to the market. I was meant to help her carry the bags but she nearly always ended up lugging most of them herself. Maybe she was hoping that someone who knew me would recognize me in the crowd. Someone who had ended up in town the same way I did. Sometimes I, too, wondered: where have they gone, all those people I used to know before? What was it about, the book in which I was a character?

What other characters were in it and what's happened to them? Or was the book only about me?

I was determined to find out, come what may. I asked Uncle Mongo, as Auntie was a woman of few words. Usually, she just told me what to do and my questions only made her sigh. She didn't have time for me. After our morning shopping expedition she would spend all day scurrying around the restaurant, working till late at night. She would go to bed much later than I, or perhaps she never even went to bed at all, as I had not once seen her sleeping. One day I heard her tell a neighbour that she hadn't slept a wink all night.

It was different with Uncle Mongo—he would spend most of the day sitting on a bench in the shade, across the street from the restaurant. He'd smoke his pipe and gaze into the distance. Or watch the customers and smile at the snatches of conversation carried by the breeze.

Then he would begin to talk. About all sorts of things, like how children come into this world. Ordinary ones are born in an ordinary way. A man loves his wife and as a token of gratitude she bears him a child. That's how he'd been born. He'd lived with his parents all their lives, so that they could raise him properly and teach him everything he needed to know and so that he would support them in their old age and carry on their work after they died. Other children, on the other hand, are brought into this world as a gift by the gods and good spirits. This happens mostly when a man loves his wife dearly, but she is too frail to bear a child herself. Then the shaman asks the ancestors to put in a good word with the spirits on behalf of the man's wife and to help him make a potent decoction. Once everything is ready, all the women from the neighbourhood gather at the house of the mother-to-be. They dance and sing in order to summon a child from the realm of the dead and the unborn. Uncle would then sing to me. He sang slowly, in a comical, high-pitched female voice:

Welcome! Welcome!
Welcome to our world!
Make the leaves green.
The jungle awaits you.
We're all here for you.
May you live in this world.
You will flourish and so we can die.
We'll hear you and lie in the ground.
You will always be happy.
Life is good, you'll see.
We await your birth.
You need fear nothing.
We will stand by you.
Welcome to our world!

Then he would be seized by a fit of coughing, and I would dash over to the restaurant to fetch him a glass of palm wine.

I would watch intently as he swilled a few drops of wine around in his mouth. Because, you see, I was very keen to find out about children like myself.

'You are unique, Myboy,' he said. He, too, had not met many people like me all his life. People who come from books are strong because they are able to survive on their own. They are much stronger and wiser than others. They can manage without a mother and a father. It doesn't take them long to discover why they have come into this world. They know what they want and pay no heed to the blockheads around them who mock and hurt them.

I asked Uncle how they happened to know this, for I was ignorant and needed him to explain every single detail.

That's when Uncle fixed me with a stare, as if searching for the right words. This went on until a mosquito landed on his nose. He stopped staring and stroked my hair.

'They learn it from the book in which they were born. And if, like you, they don't remember their story, they keep looking until they find it. In books, in newspapers, in the streets, in the branches of the trees and in the wind.'

That evening I went to bed late. I heard Uncle and Auntie murmuring well into the night. Unable to sleep, I kept thinking about other children my age, the ones I got to know in our neighbourhood. Their sweating faces, so full of joy, appeared before me. They never believed what I told them. They laughed at me, said that I was off my head, or that they felt sorry for me. I forgave them their ignorance. And I fell asleep happy.

A few days later Uncle came to see me with a mysterious smile playing about his lips. He brought me the best news of my life: a few days from now I would start going to school! The idea had never occurred to me. I was so glad that Uncle Mongo and Auntie had put me up although they didn't have money to spare. I couldn't believe my luck. Soon I would learn how to read and then I'd read all the books in the world. I would find my story!

My teacher was surprisingly young, turning men's heads when she walked down the street. I thought teachers had to be older, for old people are wiser. But there you go. On the other hand, I could picture her as a mother. My classmates were a different matter though—they showed their stupidity right from the start and treated me as a laughing stock.

The first thing we did in class was introduce ourselves.

'So what's your name, my boy?' the teacher asked when she reached the last desk, where I was sitting.

'Myboy,' I replied, perhaps too loudly, proud of my very first answer.

The whole class roared with laughter. They almost fell out of their desks as they shrieked like laughing hyenas and banged their exercise books.

When the classes were over I went to the school office to ask if I could use the mission library. The teacher nodded and gave me a lollipop.

'Will I also find a book about myself there?' I asked, so excited that I felt my heart pounding in my temples.

'Don't worry, you will find everything there.'

Now I knew things would work out fine. If everything was in there, it couldn't be hard to find the right book. Even if it was the last one I would read. From that day, I spent every free minute I had in the library of the Don Bosco Mission. Waiting for me there were shelves crammed with old books and journals imported from France or maybe even further afield. There might have been as many as a hundred. Their pages, damp and mouldy, were often stuck together. At first it took me a long time to work my way through the first pages of the paperback novels. I browsed them gingerly, looking for familiar words—looking for myself, for a story that would help me recall and reveal the truth about my past.

After school I would shut myself in the library and browse, steadily reading through almost a whole shelf. One day, in a slim volume, I found a boy who was my spitting image. He thought in exactly the same way as I do. He walked through a desolate landscape all alone, looking for his parents. I devoured these pages, thrilled, breathless—this book was about me! I found the god who had created me. I found my story!

I couldn't wait to get to the part describing my arrival in Douala. What might lie ahead for me in this world? I skipped entire paragraphs. I kept reading after dark, making use of the fluorescent light from the shop across the street. Finally, I reached the last page. But it ended in midsentence. The only thing that followed was an advertisement on the back cover. I sifted through every other volume in the library but couldn't find any paperback with the next instalment of my story.

Devastated, at home I didn't return Uncle's greeting or eat my supper. But as morning arrived, I suddenly felt better. I grabbed a doughnut from the table and bounded out, to be among people. To look for my story. To discover who I am.